S   MCHARDY is   musician, broadcast   history and folklore.   history degree from Edinburgh University in the 1970s he has found ongoing inspiration and stimulus in Scotland's dynamic story and music traditions. His research has led him far beyond his native land and he has lectured and performed in many different parts of the world. Whether telling stories to children or lecturing to adults, Stuart's enthusiasm and love of his material make him an entertaining and stimulating speaker.

His own enthusiasm and commitment have led to him re-interpreting much of the history, mythology and legends of early Western Europe. Combining the roles of scholar and performer gives McHardy an unusually clear insight into tradition and he sees connections and continuities that others may have missed. As happy singing an old ballad as analysing ancient legends, he has held such diverse positions as Director of the Scots Language Resource Centre and President of the Pictish Arts Society. He lives in Edinburgh with the lovely Sandra and they have one son, Roderick.

By the same author

Strange Secrets of Ancient Scotland (Lang Syne Publishers, 1989)

Tales of Whisky and Smuggling (Lochar, 1992)

The Wild Haggis an the Greetin-faced Nyaff (Scottish Children's Press, 1995)

Scotland: Myth, Legend and Folklore (Luath Press, 1999)

Edinburgh and Leith Pub Guide (Luath Press, 2000)

Scots Poems to be read aloud (Editor) (Luath Press, 2001)

Tales of Whisky and Smuggling (House of Lochar, 2002)

The Quest for Arthur (Luath, 2002)

The Quest for the Nine Maidens (Luath Press, 2003)

MacPherson's Rant and other tales of the Scottish Fiddle (Birlinn, 2004)

The Silver Chanter and other tales of Scottish Piping (Birlinn, 2004)

School of the Moon: the Scottish cattle raiding tradition (Birlinn, 2004)

On the Trail of Scotland's Myths and Legends (Luath Press, 2005)

The Well of the Heads and other Clan Tales (Birlinn, 2005)

Luath Storyteller: Tales of the Picts (Luath, 2005)

On the Trail of the Holy Grail (Luath, 2006)

The White Cockade and other Jacobite Tales (Birlinn, 2006)

Luath Storyteller: Tales of Edinburgh Castle (Luath, 2007)

Luath Storyteller Series
Tales of Loch Ness

STUART McHARDY

Luath Press Limited

EDINBURGH

www.luath.co.uk

First published 2009

ISBN 978-1-906307-59-2

The paper used in this book is recyclable. It is made
from low chlorine pulps produced in a low energy,
low emission manner from renewable forests.

Printed and bound by The Charlesworth Group,
Wakefield

Typeset in 10.5 point Sabon by
3btype.com

contents

introduction

OCH NESS IS SCOTLAND'S best known Loch. At over 20 miles long, a mile wide and around 700 feet at its deepest, it is the largest body of inland water in Scotland and forms one section of the Caledonian Canal, which at the time it was started in 1803 was considered a major and innovative engineering feat. It took 17 years to complete, and a further phase of building had to be undertaken in the 1840s to complete the original design by Thomas Telford. It is of course also the home of the least threatening monster in the history of mankind – Nessie. Even the name suggests a cuddly, rather than carnivorous, beastie! The ongoing fascination of whether or not there is some kind of strange, prehistoric creature living in the murky depths of the loch continues to attract visitors from all over the world to this area at the very heart of the beautiful Scottish Highlands. But Nessie is hardly the only story we have, even if the earliest mention of such a creature is nearly 1,500 years old.

The area is full of stories because, like most

of the Scottish Highlands – now mainly occupied by a combination of heather, fir trees, grouse and deer – this was an area where people lived for thousands of years. That is till they were forced off their land by the greed of a small section of the population, whose ancestral links to the land, and their kin, were no match for the lure of money and status in the context of a British state that had deliberately destroyed the ancient way of life of the Highland clans in the 18th century. That way of life, though now long gone, has left us a great deal of cultural treasure. For Loch Ness, sitting as it does in the heart of the Scottish Highlands, was always a place of importance. At one end, Pictish kings – though the term king is perhaps not a good fit for these leaders of amalgamated warrior tribes – lived at the north end, while to the south of the line of lochs running to the south-west was the great ritual site of Kilmartin, home to the Scottish tribes who, like the Picts, had been in Scotland since long before even the idea of recorded history.

The peoples who lived in Scotland before the Christian monks arrived had no writing but this did not mean that they were either ignorant or savage, though in battle their ferocity was well known. What held those ancient societies together was story. Story was used to pass on knowledge, not just of the ancestors but of the natural world, of how to live together, of how to interact with the environment and how to be a decent human being. In short, story provided the children of the ancient tribes with their education, their self-awareness and their understanding of the world they inhabited.

Some of the stories in this wee volume originated in those far off times, told around hearth fires by the light of flickering oil lamps, while others are much more recent, telling of the struggles that have always been part of Highland life.

All however have one thing in common. They are part of the very fibre of Scottish culture; a culture that has encompassed a range of languages and a variety of different societies, sometimes warring with each other and sometimes working with each other. Societies in which the great beauty and dangerous weather of the Highlands were matched with an awareness of how to survive, and even flourish, in an environment which can turn wild and dangerous in an instant.

For those outside the Highlands the people

too were often seen as wild and dangerous, but as these varied stories show they were people much the same as others, though tempered by their environment in ways that made them unique. Long after the warrior-based raiding societies of most of the rest of Europe had disappeared and people lived a more structured and less free life, the old ways carried on in the Highlands. To this day the stunning beauty of the Scottish Highlands attracts visitors from all over the world, many of whom can trace their ancestry back to the people who once roamed the glens and straths of this part of the world. Many of them have traces of the longing for their own land that accompanied so many Highlanders as they were dispersed across the globe.

Some people see wilderness in the Scottish Highlands but truth to tell, there is no real wilderness here, and if there is it is man made. For centuries beyond number people lived on this land and utilised every part of it in their day to day lives, with the possible exception of the high plateaus where little, if anything, lives or grows. It was those day to day lives that gave rise to the stories here presented; stories of the people who lived and loved around the shores of what is now one of the world's best known locations. That may be down to Nessie, wherever (and whatever) she is, but the people of Loch Ness-side have a story to tell that is as rich and varied as any people in the world. Here is just some of that story. Enjoy.

Stuart McHardy
Din Eidyn 2009

the origin of the name

WELLS HAVE ALWAYS BEEN important and where Loch Ness now sits, there used to be a particularly fine one a long time ago. No matter how dry the weather got, the well always ran clear and strong. Everyone knew how important this well was and it was imperative that every time anyone drew water from it, they replaced the great slab of stone that covered it. It was said that the spring had been blessed by Daly the Druid, and that the waters of the spring were good for all that ails humans. It was Daly that had first placed the stone over the well and had instructed the local people that they must always replace the capstone after drawing water. He had left with an ominous warning. 'The day on which my command is disregarded, desolation will overtake the land.'

Everyone knew what had to be done and, though no one knew what would happen if the druid's instructions were not followed, they were all sure that it would not be a good thing, and no one had any intention of ever finding out.

Such was the power of the druid's words that it became a matter of course, over many generations, that everyone replaced the capstone on the well when they drew water. However, one fateful day the pattern changed. A young lass, not long a mother, who lived close to the well, came in the gloaming to get water to cook the evening meal for herself and her man. It was late in the evening and she had taken off the stone, drawn water in her leather bucket and was just about to replace the capstone when she heard her baby crying at the fireside, where she had left her back in the house. The child sounded as if she was in distress and, reacting as mothers do, the lass grabbed her bucket and ran back to the house. In truth the baby had just been dreaming, woke up to find itself alone and was simply crying for her mother. As the lass took the disgruntled bairn on her knee and sang to it, she forgot all about the capstone of the well. As the light of the day faded and the darkness of the night came on, the waters of the well began to rise. Slowly at first, but with increasing force, the waters surged up and out.

The poor lass and her child were amongst the first to be drowned but the waters kept coming and coming. Soon the great strath was entirely flooded and the humans and animals were almost wiped out. One of the survivors fleeing up the hill called as he ran 'Loch a-nis! Loch a-nis!' which means 'There is a loch now!' and the old people always said that this is how the loch got its name.

a drastic mistake

ILCHUMEIN, THE OLD NAME for Fort Augustus, is nowadays thought to be a reference to the early Christian saint, Cummein. However local people long talked of another origin of the place name. It concerned a chief of the Cumming clan, who were based around Loch Lochy, the next of the lochs that are strung through the Great Glen. Now it is said that in those distant times that the chiefs of the clans had a rather unfortunate privilege. It was known as the *mercheta mulierum* and basically, it gave the chief the right to spend the first night of a marriage in bed with the new bride! Now this sounds highly unlikely to have existed among the close kin groups of the clans, but it was something that existed under the rigid feudal system in England and elsewhere on the continent, where it was called *droite de seigneur*, and it may well have been something that the Cummings had heard of and wanted to see if they could get away with.

At that time, back in the 14th century, the chief of the Cummings was living in Inverlochy

Castle and he had two sons. On hearing that a
local man, a Mackenzie, was about to be
married, the chief's sons arrived at the wedding
feast and declared that they were there to
exercise their father's right to the *mercheta
mulierum*. Being young and foolhardy, if not
downright arrogant young men, they demanded
this disgusting right of tribute, somehow –
probably because of their positions as the chief's
sons – expecting that Mackenzie would accede
to their wishes.

They did not know their man, and it might
be fair to say that they did not know very much.
To arrive at a wedding, when all the immediate
family and friends of both bride and groom were
in attendance, with such a request was, to put it
mildly, a bit daft! At first Mackenzie simply
could not believe his ears. They were asking
what? To sleep with his wife as their right!
Well in the Highlands of Scotland there was
always one right that could be called on
whenever disputes arose, and that was the sword.
Yet Mackenzie, despite his fury and out of the
natural respect he felt towards their father as the
chief of the Cumming clan, told the young men
not to be so silly and that it would be advisable

if they left. This, of course, the young Cummings took as a direct insult and, putting their hands on their swords, they declared that they would exercise their right, come what may.

Now young men are often stubborn and foolish, and this is what leads to so much pointless violence even today, but these two must have been blinded by arrogance, or perhaps one or both of them had had an eye on the bride for a while. Mackenzie told them to go once more and the brothers drew their swords. Mackenzie was not wearing a sword – he was getting married after all – but there was no shortage of arms at the feast and a sword was thrown to him as the brothers came at him. Within seconds, half a dozen of Mackenzie's kin were at his side, their swords drawn too. All of them hoped that this would make the Cummings see the stupidity of their actions, but their blood was up and they refused to back down. Raised as warriors since infancy, they scorned fear and came at the groom and his kin. The outcome was never in doubt and within minutes the two brothers lay dead on the ground. The whole of the wedding company was roused in fury at this ridiculous and disgusting turn of events and it was not long before someone said that the lads could hardly have tried to exercise this obnoxious act without the support, and maybe even the encouragement, of their father. And if it had been tried once would it not be tried again, next time by the chief himself?

Words were spoken then that served to inflame the gathering even further and it was only a matter of minutes before those who had not come armed were rushing to get their own weapons. Their intention was simple. By their actions Cummings and his sons had shown themselves utterly unfit to be the leaders of any clan. They would go to Inverlochy Castle and drive Cummings out of the country. As they headed to the castle word of what was happening spread like wildfire and by the time they had reached Inverlochy their numbers had swollen to hundreds. Every one was disgusted and appalled at this evil act. Now Cummings did have a few loyal supporters and they tried to defend the castle, but as the word spread more and more armed men were seen to be approaching the castle.

Soon such a vast crowd had gathered that the chief realised his only hope of surviving was

to give in to the crowd's will and leave his
ancestral home. So he surrendered and was
escorted from the clan lands with just a handful
of followers. In just one day he had lost his
beloved sons and the ancient home of his fathers.
It was a broken-hearted man who headed off
north with only what he and his meagre band
could carry with them. He did not want to go
any further from his beloved home than he had
to and stopped to set up his new home on the
southern banks of Loch Ness. Soon after that
he died, no longer having the will to live, and
after he was buried. The place was given the
name of Kilchumein because it was there that
the one time chief of the Cummings was laid
to rest.

the early saints

OW IN THE FAR DISTANT PAST in the
Scottish Highlands, deer were
considered special creatures. They
were known throughout the
mountains and glens as *crodh nan
Cailleach*, the cattle of the Cailleach, and though
in most surviving stories about her the Cailleach
is a great and ugly hag, there is no doubt that she
was, in times long gone, a Mother Goddess
figure. There are many different stories linking
deer to ancient ritual, some of them involving
women who changed into deer and back again.
They occur in many of the traditional tales that
were told in the clachans round the hearth fires.
The great Finn MacCoul, leader of the legendary
Fianna, had a wife turned into a deer by an evil
druid, and the son she gave birth to was Oisin,
the poet of the Fianna, whose name means fawn.
They occur on Pictish Symbol stones and even
older carvings in different parts of the country.
Originally representative of a goddess, deer were
an integral part of ancient Highland culture,
so it should be no surprise that when the men
of the cross came into the Highlands they

too would be associated with deer. While it was declared Christian policy to take over as much of earlier religious practice as possible – to help convince the people of the benefit of the new ways – some of the early saints seemed to have been particularly involved with deer.

saint finan

AINT FINAN, WHO WAS a close
companion of Columba's, like
his compatriot spent some time
spreading the word of the new
religion around the area of Loch
Ness. Time and again he returned
to this part of the world from Iona and even
as the years came on him and he grew infirm,
he continued to try and spread the tenets of the
religion he so believed in. No longer could he
walk miles over trackless lands as he had done
as a young man. Now he was forced to travel
on horseback, his old and weary limbs incapable
of covering the distances he still wanted to cross.
One time he was heading down Loch Ness
towards Loch Lochy, where he and some
companions had raised a church made of wattle
and daub and planted some crops. He was
looking forward to joining his companions
and maybe not paying enough attention to the
ground he was crossing. In those far off times
such tracks as did exist were often rough indeed
and as he passed along, his horse stepped into a
hole in the track. Down it went with a great

cracking noise. The horse screamed wildly and the old monk was thrown to the ground, luckily well clear of the animal. There was little he could do for the poor animal. If he tried to get close to slit its throat with the knife he carried to cut his meat he was liable to be hit by its thrashing legs, or even bitten by the tormented beast. As he looked on pityingly at the stricken animal it began to dawn on Finan that he too was in deep trouble. There was no way he could walk to Loch Lochy and he realised that the track he was on was not one that was well-trodden. Such was his infirmity, if no one came soon he knew well that, like the horse, there was little if any chance that he would ever escape from this place. So, as such men do in such situations, he knelt and prayed.

He had not been praying long when suddenly he felt something warm and wet nuzzling his cheek. He opened his eyes and turned to look. There, standing beside him was a magnificent red stag. Behind it he could see that the horse with the broken leg was lying peacefully on the ground. He looked at the stag in wonder. It seemed to be trying to tell him something. He looked again at the horse. Its leg was

obviously broken under it, but no longer was
it thrashing about in pain. Finan was mystified
but as he looked again at the stag, the
magnificent animal bowed its head and bent its
knees. What was this? Was the animal getting
ready to take him on its back? This was
unbelievable. But then he remembered the
power of prayer and, thanking God profusely,
the old monk got stiffly to his feet and clambered
onto the back of the great red beast. Taking a
farewell look at the horse that was lying calmly
and quietly on the ground, Finan and the deer
headed south.

The stag seemed to know where it was going
and only a few hours later the monks at the little
settlement on Loch Lochy were astounded to see
their ancient mentor coming along the road on
the back of a stag. Reaching his companions, the
old monk slid off the stag's back and patted the
animal gently on the head. It then shook its head,
let out a roar, turned and bounded off into the
forest. Turning to the open-mouthed monks,
Finan spread his arms, shrugged and said, 'Well,
we all know the Lord moves in mysterious ways.'

saint cummein

NOTHER SAINT WHO WAS active around the waters of Loch Ness was Saint Cummein. He was based near what is now Fort Augustus, originally known as Kilchumein after the saint himself who was Abbot of Iona. Back in the sixth century much of the country here was wild and uncultivated and when Cummein came with a group of monks to set up a church on the banks of the loch there was much to be done. Initially a church had to be built, then houses to live in. Then Cummein knew they would have to grow grain to sustain the community in the future. Most of the monks he had with him were used to the religious life and some had even joined the church as a way of avoiding the arduous work that farming entailed in those far off days. However, Cummein was not a man who was frightened by the idea of hard work and he set the monks to breaking the ground around the church site. It was hard and dirty work and some of the monks were none too pleased to be doing it. They had joined the Abbot to spread the word of God, not to break and till the soil!

They wanted to be out and about preaching to the pagan tribes of the area; that was what they had signed up for.

One particular monk, who came from a family of chiefs back in his native Ireland, was particularly upset at having to labour like everyone else.

'If we have need of ploughed land, should the good Lord not have provided us with it?' he asked of Cummein. In truth his attitude may well have been brought about by the fact that his soft hands were blistered from hard work and his back was sore from the bending the work entailed.

'If that is what you think, so be it,' replied the saint 'The Lord will provide but you will not feed from the crops grown here.'

The monk and his companions took this as justification to down tools and went off to the loch to try and catch some fish – that was much easier work to fill their bellies. They were successful and that night they fed well.

The next morning they arose and came out from their huts to see a wondrous sight. There before them was the saint himself with four deer, great many-horned stags, hitched to a plough.

At his command they began to pull the plough through the freshly turned ground. Several of the monks fell to their knees and began to pray. Others felt ashamed that they had turned their back on their leader and mentor. As midday approached, a couple of the monks went to the saint to offer him some of the fish they had caught and cooked but he refused to take even a bite.

All day long Cummein stood directing the deer in some unfathomable way, occasionally running to help if one of the ploughs snagged on a boulder or a root. All day the deer crossed and re-crossed the patch of land till, as night began to fall, the saint released them from their harness and thanked them. The stately creatures bowed their heads briefly and headed off into the forest. This was observed by all the monks, some of whom were now feeling deeply ashamed of their earlier actions.

In the middle of the night, unable to sleep because of how guilty they felt, four of the monks arose and went to the barn where the plough had been left. They had agreed they should try to do something to help Cummein get the land ploughed and the crops grown.

They looked in the barn, a very rough structure that had been thrown up a day or so earlier, but there was no plough there. Hearing a noise from the field where the deer had been active earlier, they went to see what it was. There by the light of the moon they could see that a great, dark, horse-like creature was carrying on the work the deer had started. As they looked on in amazement the monks realised that this was the *each-uisge*, the wild water-horse of Loch Ness! Again they fell to their knees and prayed at the wonder they were seeing. On and on the supernatural creature went, ploughing the last of the land that had been readied and finishing what had been begun by the deer. Then the saint came forward – the monks had noticed him watching all that was going on – and unhitched the plough. He blessed the strange creature, who turned to go. However before it returned to the deep, cold waters of Loch Ness, it went into the hut where the monk who had been the first to complain lay asleep. His horrified companions could only look on as the horse reappeared with the recalcitrant monk on his back and headed straight into the Loch with its human cargo, who was never seen again.

SONG OF THE DEER

F COURSE THE MOST FAMOUS of the saints associated with Loch Ness is Columba, who came over from Ireland to Iona in the 560's. He was very aware of the politics of his time and decided that he needed to try and convince the King of the Picts, Bridei, that the new religion was the way of the future. It was a long journey from Iona to Bridei's court at Inverness, and once they had reached the mainland they had to walk the rest of the way. It was not long after they had come to southern Loch Ness that they realised they were being followed by a heavily armed band of men. Columba had no idea if these warriors had been sent by Bridei himself, one of the other chiefs of the Pictish tribes, or were even under the direction of some druid or druidess. Now in the early days of the church there were many martyrs and it seems likely that there were a few of the Christians who could acquit themselves well in battle. Columba himself had been involved in a battle with fellow Christians back in his native Ireland, a situation that had led directly to his exile to Scotland. However he was neither in a mood to be martyred nor to stand and fight.

'Fear not, my sons. We will be safe under the Lord's protection as long as you do as I tell you.' This was said with a gentle smile and his steady demeanour calmed down the more frightened of the monks. 'Come around me in a circle and when I say so, I want you all to start singing the new prayer we learned last week.'

The monks were taken aback. Surely if they started singing they would alert the warriors to their position. The Picts would hear them and fall upon them like ravaging wolves. This seemed madness. Surely Columba could not be serious!

'Fear not,' said Columba, still smiling. 'Come on now and join me in the chant and I promise you all will be well.'

So there in the forest adjoining the great waters of Loch Ness, Columba and his small band of monks started to chant. Less than half a mile from where they stood, the Pictish warriors heard a noise.

'What is that?' asked the leader of the war-band, as they stopped to listen.

'Ach, it is nothing but the belling of some

stags in the woods,' one of his companions spoke up. 'Let's press on ahead and catch up on with these damned Christians. They must be a fair bit ahead of us if the stags are undisturbed.'

And on they pressed, coming close to where Columba and the monks stood chanting, but all they heard was the sound of belling stags as the monks lustily sang the prayer known ever after as the Song of the Deer.

a strange meeting

T WASN'T ONLY DEER that Columba ran into when in the area around Loch Ness. Another time he was on his way to Inverness, and he and his companions were trying to find a way across the deep waters of the loch, when they came across a group of people near the shores who were busy burying the body of a young man. As they stood and watched the proceedings, one of Columba's monks, who spoke Pictish, asked a bystander how the young lad had died. He listened a while then turned to Columba and informed the saint that the poor youth had been swimming in the loch when a gigantic snake-like creature had come up from the depths and taken a great bite out of his side. The lad had just managed to swim to the shore before he died.

Columba was busy looking over the loch as the monk spoke. Spotting a small boat on the far side, he said to the monk, 'Look over yonder. There is a boat that could carry us over the waters of this loch. Just you swim over and row it back to us.'

The monk looked long and hard at the saint.

Had he been listening? Didn't he understand about the ominous creature in the water? However, he knew that Columba had power over many things, including the weather and almost every creature on the planet. So with total faith in his leader he took off his robe and waded out into the cold waters of the loch. He was only a few yards out into the loch, swimming towards the boat, when 100 yards ahead of him the head of a monstrous eel-like creature broke the surface of the water. At once it headed towards the swimming man.

The funeral party saw what was happening and many of them began to yell and point. Others fell to their knees and wept. Even some of Columba's monks fell to their knees and began to implore the Lord to save their friend from this dreadful monster. The great scaly creature bore down on the young monk as Columba calmly watched. Then, just as the evil-looking creature seemed about to strike, Columba formed the shape of the cross in the air with his right hand and called out in his powerful voice, 'Go no further here, nor touch the man. Turn now, turn and go back whence you came!'

The creature, which had reared up to strike at the swimming monk, seemed to stop absolutely still in the water. It was as if it had been pierced by a spear. The upper half of its slimy and scaly body stood straight out of the water and its great ugly head turned to look at the saint. To those watching it seemed that the great monster hung in the air forever before it shook its head, let out a high-pitched squeal, turned and dived back below the waves of Loch Ness. At a sign from Columba the monk, who had been treading water as the foul beast had approached, continued swimming to the other side and fetched the boat back. Soon the saint and his companions were over the loch and carried peacefully on their way towards Inverness and nothing more was seen of the monstrous beast. Well, not until well over 1,000 years later, though nowadays we call her Nessie.

loch ness weather

OW LOCH NESS IS VERY DEEP and very
long. With the mountains looming
close on both sides, it is a place where
the weather can turn pretty wild.
There was one time however when the
weather here was of a very particular kind.

It happened not long after Columba had
first come to see King Bridei at Inverness
that the king, having heard this stranger
with his new religion was approaching his fort,
ordered the great wooden gates to be shut
against him. Columba had one of his monks
hammer on the doors with his staff but nothing
happened. Ordering the monk to stand back
Columba went up to the door, made the sign
of the cross on the wood and laid both his hands
on the great doors. Inside, the bolts on the other
side slid back of their own accord and the vast
wooden doors swung open to allow the priest
to enter into the fort. This exhibition of
supernatural power greatly impressed King
Bridei but did not go down too well with the
king's druid Broichan, who deeply resented this
show of magic powers.

From the moment of the saint's arrival there was ill-feeling between the two of them and this was made worse by Columba becoming aware that Broichan had a female slave who came from Dalriada, the land of the Scots in Argyll. Columba was heavily involved with the Scots, regularly visited their capital of Dunadd, and in the presence of the king Bridei, asked the druid to set the woman free. The druid simply laughed at him.

At that the priest said to him 'Know, O Broichan, and be assured that if thou refuse to set this captive free, as I desire thee, thou shall die suddenly before I take my departure again from this province.'

Again the druid just laughed, though truth to tell he was scared that the priest might just have the power to do as was threatened. At that Columba took his leave of the king, gathered his monks and set off towards the River Ness to make his way south. On reaching the river, he knelt by the water's edge, stuck his hand into the river and pulled out a white pebble. Holding it up he said, 'Behold this white pebble, by which God will effect the cure of many diseases among this heathen nation.'

He then told the monks that even as he spoke, back in Inverness the Druid Broichan had been attacked by an angel from Heaven who a smashed the glass the druid was drinking from and left him gasping for breath on the floor. He went on, 'If we wait a while, the king's messengers will come and ask that we return to see if we can help the Druid for he is clearly dying.'

Sure enough it was less than an hour before two Pictish warriors on horseback came riding up to the monks and asked Columba to go back to the court to help the druid who had fallen very ill.

'I will send two of my monks with you and they shall cure the druid, but I must be heading home,' he replied.

Then, turning to the two nearest monks, he told them they were to go back to Inverness, taking the pebble he had just pulled from the river. There, once the Druid agreed to free the slave girl, they were to put the stone into a cup of water and give it to Broichan to drink. 'However,' he told them, 'if he refuses to free the girl, do not help him, and he will die instantly.'

The monks did as they were told and headed

back to Inverness. There they told Broichan that he would be cured by the power of the great Columba but only if he agreed to free the girl. Broichan, aware of just how close he was to death, agreed at once. The stone was immersed in a cup of water and the druid drank the water. All at once his symptoms left him and he was as healthy as he had ever been. The two monks then left, taking the Scots girl with them, and followed after the priest.

Now you may think that this would have softened Broichan's attitude towards Columba, but not a bit of it. On the saint's next visit to Inverness, when he had come all the way up Loch Ness by boat, he realised that Broichan still resented him. One day just before he was about to leave, Broichan asked him what time he would be setting sail on Loch Ness.

'Three days from now, God willing,' replied the saint.

'Well, we will see,' replied Broichan with a cold smile, 'for I think that the weather will be against you.'

'I put my trust in the good Lord and have no need to fear the weather,' Columba said.

Three days later, as the priest and his

followers headed off to the loch, the weather began to turn. The sky darkened, the wind blew up and soon squalls of rain were whipping along the surface of the loch. The wind grew stronger and stronger and the day darkened even more, all as a result of the spells Broichan had been so busy casting for the previous three days. The waves on the loch rose higher and higher and the wind began to howl, coming straight up the loch towards where Columba and his friends were standing. There was no way that any boat could set sail against that wind and it seemed clear that anyone trying would be capsized in an instant by the surging waves.

Columba knelt and prayed briefly, then rose and walked calmly to the small boat that was rocking wildly by the bank where it was moored. Stepping in, he summoned his monks to follow him and ordered the sails to be raised at once. The crowd who had come to see him off, and those who knew what Broichan had been planning, all looked on in wonder. Was the man mad? The weather was worsening by the second! However as soon as the sails were up Columba stood up in the prow of the boat and the little craft sailed out straight into the teeth of the wind at a speed no one there could believe.

Straight as an arrow the boat raced across Loch Ness in the face of the howling gale. After just a minute or two, the wind began to slacken then shift and at last it veered around totally, till it was filling the sails of the holy man's boat and driving him on his journey home. After that Broichan though better of tangling with Columba. Or so the story goes.

saint merchard and his miracles

SCOTLAND HAS MANY SAINTS who are not known elsewhere but seem to have had long held a place in the hearts and minds of the people, and Loch Ness-side is no different in this respect. Here, around Glenmoriston, there was one particular saint to whom the people paid great veneration. This was St Merchard and it is said that he had come to the west from the foothills of the Grampian mountains. Some say he had been raised at a place called Tolmauds, a few miles to the north of Kincardine O'Neill on the banks of the Dee, and had been taken under the wing of that earlier saint, Ternan, who, based at Banchory, was active in the north-east of Scotland long before the arrival of the Irish priest Columba on Iona. When he was ordained a priest, Merchard had headed west and ended up in Strathglass, to the west of Loch Ness. While it has been written of him that he went to Rome and was made a bishop

by Pope Gregory, the local traditions tell of a
different tale.

It seems he was living in Strathglass with two
fellow priests. Their life was one of hard work
and contemplation, of simplicity and prayer.
One day it is said he was out on the hillside
praying, when his attention was caught by a
cow that was acting strangely. It was a white
cow and it was standing stock still just looking
directly at a tree. He watched it for a few
minutes and the beast didn't move, apart
from occasionally flicking its tail. Later the
same day he noticed that the cow still had not
moved. The same thing happened the following
day, and the day after that. This went on for
several days and Merchard was intrigued.
He noted that the cow did not seem to be eating
anything but appeared as healthy and well-fed
as the other cattle. And it was always the same
tree that it stood before.

Being as devout as he was, Merchard
wondered if this might indeed be some kind
of a sign from God, so he decided to have a
good look around the tree. He had longed for
a sign ever since he had joined the priesthood;
a sign that he had chosen the right path in

service of the Lord. There appeared to be nothing special about the tree, it was just like all the others around it but, fascinated by the cow's incredible concentration, he decided to dig up the ground at the foot of the tree. He had not dug down very far when he hit something hard. Scrabbling in the earth he found a bell, then another and another! Once he brushed the earth from them, he realised these beautiful bronze objects appeared brand new, shining as if they had just been made that very hour. When he shook one of them and its clapper hit the bell, the tone was deep and thrilling. Surely this was the sign he had been waiting for.

Somehow he just knew what had to be done. He gave a bell each to his two companions and told them, 'Go forth from here, and wherever your bell rings for the third time untouched, that is where you should raise your church and spread the word of the Lord.'

One of them went east and founded the church at Glenconvinth; the other travelled west and ended up building his church at Broadford on the Isle of Skye. Merchard himself headed south towards Glenmoriston. On top of the hill – for long after called Suidhe Mherchierd or Merchard's Seat – his bell rang for the first time. The second time it was at Fuaran Mhercheird, Merchard's Well at Ballintombuie, and the third time was where the old burying ground of Glenmoriston stands. Here he raised his church Clachan Mhercheird. Soon he was spreading the Christian doctrine through the hills and up and down the Great Glen formed by Loch Ness, Loch Lochy and Loch Linnhe.

As is always the case with such early missionaries, he acquired a reputation for sanctity and in time, after he himself had gone to meet his maker, he became the patron saint of the glen. However as the patron saint of Glenmoriston he was more than just a general beneficent being to whom the locals would address their prayers. No, Merchard was much more directly involved with the descendants of those who had been his parishioners back in the fifth century.

Long ago there was a custom that when a tenant died, his best horse went to the landowner, and if there was no horse then its value in sheep or cattle had to be substituted. This was probably based on an ancient clan tradition that was corrupted in the times when the land passed from the ownership of the clan, held by the chief on their behalf, to the laird or landowner, often the descendants of chiefs who had taken personal ownership. The laird who had acquired the lands of Glenmoriston was one MacPhatrick, and it is the nature of humans that there are always those who are more than ready to do the bidding of those they consider their betters. Just such a one was MacPhatrick's factor.

And so it was that one time in the 18th century, a poor woman was left alone when her husband died and the laird's factor came to call. She and her husband had always got by but possessed little other than a few sheep. The factor demanded that she hand over almost her entire wee flock and drove them off, leaving the widow facing a life of extreme poverty and hardship. That very night as the factor lay sleeping, he was startled into consciousness as a great voice boomed, 'I am Merchard of the miracles, passing homeward in the night. You go tell MacPhatrick that the widow's sheep will never bring him any good.'

After spending the rest of the night wide awake and in a cold sweat, in the morning the terrified factor scurried off to tell his master

what had happened, and such was the state
he was in that MacPhatrick himself thought
he should pay heed to the warning from the
saint. So it was that later that same day the
poor widow was surprised and delighted to
have her sheep returned to her and when the
story came out that it was because of the saint's
intervention there were many candles lit to Saint
Merchard in the local church that year.

MERCHARD'S BELL

HE BELL THAT HAD BROUGHT the saint to the area long outlasted the saint himself and was still a fixture until around 1870. It was used as a miracle cure for all sorts of diseases and after the stone built church at Clachan Mhercheird fell into disuse in the 17th century, the bell was simply kept on an old tombstone in the kirkyard. All people had to do to gain benefit from its powers was to touch it. Like many another ancient saint's bell in Scotland it had the power of flight, for no matter where it was taken it would always find its way back to Clachan Mhercheird. However, it had been involved in its share of miracles down the centuries since Merchard first came. It was known to ring out whenever a funeral approached the old burial ground of the kirkyard and those who knew of such things said it sang out a message, in Gaelic of course, that translated as 'Home, home, to thy lasting place of rest.' The bell was also supposed to have the power of floating on water, but the locals long remembered a saying that had come from the saint regarding this aspect of the bell. He said, 'I am Merchard from across the land. Keep ye my sufferings in your remembrance and see that you do not for a wager place this bell in the pool to swim.' So while it was believed that the bell could swim, nobody ever dared test it!

However the bell's capacity to ring of itself could prove helpful. It was one dark night as winter approached that the people of the clachan were all aroused from their beds in the middle of the night by the bell ringing long and loud. Dressing quickly, people came running from all of the houses in the wee village and headed to the kirkyard. Everyone assumed that something had gone wrong and that the bell was being rung to summon them. Some of them were looking around to see if any of their neighbours' houses were on fire. Others had grabbed their weapons, usually kept close to hand in the thatch of the standard black houses of the Highlands, thinking that they were being raided. But no house was on fire and no one was shouting about raiders. Soon the entire adult population of the clachan were gathered at the kirkyard and there, by the light of the torches many of them were carrying, they saw

a dreadful sight. Close to the tombstone where
the bell rested was the body of a man, a stranger.
He was dead but the blood had not even begun
to congeal in the gaping wound in his chest.
He had obviously been killed only minutes
before and here in the ancient holy graveyard
of Clachan Mhercheird. This was a bloody
and sacrilegious act.

The men of the place, many of whom were
no strangers to violent death themselves, realised
that whoever had done this foul deed was close
to hand. So they spread out and within minutes
found another stranger hiding in a ditch.
When he was dragged back to the kirkyard,
there in the light of the torches all could see his
blood-drenched clothes. There was little doubt
of his guilt and it was a short time before he
was hanged, but as to what had caused the
quarrel that led to the killing, he never said.

The bell remained a noted fixture in
Glenmoriston until around 1870 when the
ancient relic disappeared forever. The locals
had no doubt that it had been taken by strangers
to the district, who had stolen it and travelled
as fast and as far away as they could. By then
of course there were railways on the land and

it seems that the speed of modern transport and the distance travelled proved too much even for the fabled powers of the bell!

loch ness waterhorse

SCOTLAND HAS MANY STORIES of *each-uisgean* – water-horses or Kelpies, supernatural creatures who made a habit of preying on humans. Always beautiful creatures, they are associated with rivers and lochs all across the country and Loch Ness has its own *each-uisge*. These beautiful creatures were dangerous in the extreme. While some of them concentrated on luring young women into their watery homes, others were happy to capture any human. Their trick was to appear as a wandering horse and induce one or more humans to climb on their backs. Then they would make straight for their watery home and dive in, their supernatural powers keeping the humans on their backs as if glued.

One time two brothers were fishing in the waters of Loch Ness. They were just boys and before they had gone out in their little skin boat their father had given them a very clear warning: 'Now lads, be very careful. Make sure that you do not get tricked by the *each-uisge*. It appears as a beautiful big golden horse with a golden

bridle all covered in precious stones, but it is
a deadly creature that will drag you into the
loch and drown you if it can. If you see a big,
golden, beautiful horse like that, turn away
and come home at once. All right now, do you
understand? Fine, go and catch us some nice
fish for our supper.'

The boys nodded, but like boys anywhere
they soon forgot what their father had told
them. In truth, they had heard about the water-
horse on many an occasion and the idea of
such a wondrous and terrifying beast no longer
worried them. They were much more concerned
with the fact that their father now trusted them
to go out on the loch on their own to fish.

They had quite a good day of it and after
catching half a dozen good-sized fish they
headed back to shore. They had just pulled
the light skin-covered boat onto the shore when
the younger one said to his brother, 'Och look,
John. What a beautiful beast.'

John turned to follow his wee brother's
pointing finger and there at the edge of the
woods, close to the shore stood a beautiful,
golden horse. It was the most wonderful thing
they had ever seen and its magnificent shiny

coat just seemed to make the heavy golden,
jewel-encrusted bridle round its head shine
even brighter. They were entranced, caught up
in the spell of the Otherworld creature, and
neither of them remembered a single word
of their father's warning only hours earlier.

The horse began to come towards them
and William moved towards it holding out his
hand, making a gentle shushing sound to keep
the horse calm, just as he had seen his father
do so often. Closer and closer horse and boy
came. At last the horse was right beside William
and only as he grabbed the bridle and began
to climb on its back did John remember his
father's words.

It was as if he could hear him calling from a
far away place, but the message was clear: This
was the water-horse they had been warned of.

'No, William, no! Don't get on its back!
That's the *each-uisge*! Stop, William, stop!'

But he was too late, for by now William
was sitting astride the handsome beast. John
ran towards his brother and as he put his
hand on the beast's coat to try and pull at
William with the other hand, he realised his
hand was stuck. Now both of them were under

the horse's power. Looking up he could see that
William looked as if he was off in a dream –
he had a great smile on his face but his eyes were
distant, as if looking at some far away thing.

John's heart was beating furiously but he
was a brave lad and he knew what he must do.
Every Highland laddie carried a *sgian dubh*, the
wee black knife, until the day he was old enough
to be given his own dirk. Quick as a flash, John
pulled the *sgian dubh* from his belt with his free
hand and sliced off his own fingers. At the sight
of the cold steel of the blade, the horse reared
up and away. Otherworld creatures cannot
bear the touch of steel and even the sight of it
terrifies them. As the horse reared, John fell
back and the beast turned and sped off with
William stuck firmly to its back. John was
terrified that the creature would head straight
into the cold waters of the loch, but before he
could try and follow it he had to do something
about his hand. The excitement was so intense
that adrenalin was pumping through his veins
and he felt virtually no pain. He knew that if
he did not do something quickly he could easily
bleed to death. Luckily he had listened better
to his mother than his father and he knew that

a plant that grew locally, the fig wort, would
keep the wound clean and hasten recovery.
So he looked around till he found some and
then, packing the leaves tight against the stubs
of his fingers, he cut a piece of cloth from his
shirt and bound his hand up tight. Only then
did he head off, following the horse's tracks
deep into the woods.

Soon he came to a house where his uncle
lived on his own. The tracks of the horse
went right past the house and off deeper into
the woods. At least the creature wasn't heading
directly for the Loch. There was no one at
his uncle's, but the wee lad went in and lifted
his uncle's great sword that he kept behind the
door – in those days it was well advised to
keep your weapons near to hand, just in case.
With the sword over his shoulder and gripping
it tight with his good hand, the brave wee lad
went on tracking the *each-uisge*, terrified to
his soul that he would be unable to do anything
to help his big brother. On and on he went,
never losing the track till the afternoon waned
and the gloaming came on. Just as the shadows
of night were beginning to grow, he came into
a clearing. There in the middle of it was the

water-horse. And on its back was William,
still with that funny, fixed look on his face,
oblivious to the horse that was nibbling at
the grass.

John sucked in his breath. Slowly, very
slowly, he moved through the trees till he was
directly behind the horse and boy. Then, taking
as much care as he could, he crept up on the
grazing animal. Closer and closer he came,
till he could hear the creature breathing. Still
William sat contentedly on the evil creature's
back. Then John made his move. With all of
his wee boy's strength he ran at the horse and
brought the heavy sword down on its neck.
Straight through its neck went the sword and
the beast toppled, sending William tumbling
into the grass.

John ran to where William was sprawled in
the grass. Lying there, William looked up at him
quizzically. 'What happened, Johnnie?' Looking
around he got to his feet, a look of puzzlement
on his face.

'William, William! You're all right, you're all
right!' shouted the wee boy, dropping the sword
and running to clasp his brother in his arms.

'I'm fine, I'm fine, Johnnie. But what

happened? Good heavens, what's wrong with your hand?' William stared at the bloody stump.

Johnnie was just about to explain when he heard a noise behind him. Turning quickly, he saw a young man with long golden hair and pale skin, dressed in very fine clothes, standing just where the evil creature had fallen. He looked around. There was no sign of the *each-uisge* at all. It had disappeared. The boys looked at the stranger.

The stranger smiled and bowed. 'Thank you, John,' he said and put forward his right hand. There, lying in the palm, were Johnnie's fingers. 'You have done me a great service this day. Now let me do a service for you. Come here,' the stranger went on.

Feeling no fear at all, the wee lad went forward.

'Now give me your hand,' said the fair stranger.

Johnnie held out his bandaged stump of a hand. Gently the stranger undid the bandage, removed the figwort leaves and somehow, Johnnie could never tell exactly how he did it, put flesh to flesh, bone to bone, and Johnnie felt his hand become whole again. It was magic.

'That,' said the stranger, 'is the very least I can do. I have been under a spell put on me by a powerful wizard to live as an *each-uisge*, apart from all my family and even my race, until some lad who had never lifted a sword before should cut off my head. You have done that for me, and I will be in your debt forever.'

hags of the hills

ONG BEFORE THE SAINTS ARRIVED with their bells and their book, there were many stories told of the Cailleachs, the hags who once were goddesses. Even after the people of Loch Ness-side were Christianized they continued to tell the stories of these fierce creatures. Now one of the clans who lived on the western shores of Loch Ness was the MacMillans. They were haunted by a particularly nasty spirit – Cailleach a' Chrathaich, the Hag of the Craach. While she hated all humans, her particular venom was always directed against those of the MacMillan clan. She was generally to be found on the high hills to the west of the Loch, where she kept her eye out for any passing man. Her favourite ploy was to approach the traveller and engage him in conversation, pretending to simply be an old woman who lived on her own in the high hills. While she was fearfully ugly, such was the courtesy of the average Highlander that he would always treat any elderly person, and particularly one of the female gender, with respect. While passing the

time in talking of the weather or the price of
cattle, which was always something Highlanders
were deeply concerned about, she would secretly
steal the man's bonnet. Such were her skills,
supernatural and otherwise, that she could
have the hat off a man's head without him
noticing. By the time he did realise that his
bonnet was gone, it was generally too late,
for once she had the bonnet and her victim
was out of sight, she would sit herself down in
the heather and begin to rub away at the bonnet.
She was a fearsomely powerful being and soon
the cloth of the best of bonnets would begin to
stretch and grow thin. As this happened, the
unsuspecting traveller would find himself
growing ever wearier till at last, just as she
rubbed a hole thorough the fabric of his bonnet,
he would fall where he stood, never to rise again.
Using this trick she had killed dozens of men,
many of them MacMillans.

One day she met Donald MacMillan of
Balmaccan, who was passing over that wild
part of the country just at Cragan na Crathaich,
the great rock of the Craach, high up in the hills.
She was sitting close to the path as he came by
and she cried out, 'A good day to you, young sir.'

With all due respect, Donald turned towards her and replied, 'Aye, it is a fine day, mother. And it seems sure to be a fine evening too.'

By this point she had stood up and was coming towards him, so he felt he should stop for a moment.

Slowly, she made her way over to him and asked, 'And what kin are you of, sir?'

This was a pretty normal question in the Highlands and Donald told her he was a Macmillan.

'Ah, just so, just so,' she said with a wee smile. 'I have known a few of your kin down the years. Well, I wish you well of your journey. Farewell.'

'A good day to you,' said Donald and turned back to head on his way, not noticing that the wily old hag had whisked the bonnet from off his head.

A few minutes later however there was one of those sudden bursts of rain that seem to come from nowhere in an instant and vanish just as quickly. As the rain drops spattered off his head, Donald quickly realised that his bonnet was gone. All at once he remembered the stories he had heard of the Cailleach a' Chrathaich.

At once he ran back to the spot he had met her.
He was a fit and able Highlander, well used to
travelling through the mountains, and it didn't
take him long to return and find the old crone
sitting by the big rock, muttering some kind of
incantation and rubbing furiously at his bonnet.

'Give me that, you evil old witch!' he cried
as he ran up and snatched at his bonnet.
She held on to it and they fell together into
the heather. Over and over they rolled as first
one, then the other got on top and tried to rip
the bonnet from the other's grasp. The old
woman had remarkable strength, but Donald
was a fit young man and at last, after what
seemed like hours, he succeeded in pulling the
bonnet from her grasp and sprang back from
her as she lay cursing in the heather. As he
turned to run from the spot, she let out a terrible
scream that turned his blood to ice water.
He shivered as her voice rang out, twisted
into horror with malice and spite and getting
louder with every syllable

'Aye, you may have got your bonnet back,
MacMillan, but it will do you little good.
Three weeks from this day at nine in the evening,
I will have my wish and you will die, die, die!'

By the time she had finished her voice was like thunder and Donald, haring off along the path, could hear every word as if she stood behind him. He didn't stop till he got home and told his wife and family of his dreadful encounter.

Enough of them knew of others who had succumbed to the malice of the Hag of the Craach for them all to be worried for him. Several of them went with Donald to see the minister to see what he could do. As always he told them firmly that they must put their faith in the Lord.

So when the fateful night came round, Donald was surrounded by his family and his neighbours. Virtually the whole community of Balmacaan was there to try and help him. Some were on their knees reading from the scriptures and others were standing, praying and holding hands in a circle around Donald in his chair. His eyes were fixed on the hands of the clock. The murmur of prayer grew louder as the hour hand made its last movement. Then, just as the first stroke of nine rang out, Donald Macmillan sat forward in his chair, gave a great gasp and fell back, dead. Despite the combined prayers of his whole community, the Cailleach a' Chrathaich had triumphed over the MacMillans once more.

It seems that Cailleach a' Chrathaich did not always get her own way though. Another supernatural female, who lived at Cragan-na-Caillich near Tornashee, was reputed to warn intended victims of Cailleach a' Chrathaich that she was lying in wait for them and was considered an altogether much milder creature. However, most such spirits were, to say the least, capable of mischief, and of course had considerable supernatural powers – even control over other creatures of the Otherworld. In the old religion, everything was believed to have its own spirit – not just trees and rivers but rocks and plants – and much of this survived in the thinking of many Highland people who were generally considered to be pious Christians. One such pious Christian was Donald Monroe of Lochletter, who was passing Cragan-na-Caillich on horseback late one evening on his way home. As he neared the rock, out came the wizened old hag and she begged him for a seat behind him on the horse. It was well known that this wild creature was very fond

of riding and Donald was not daft enough to
let any of her kind sit behind him. 'Ach fine,
mother. I will give you a ride on my fine horse,
but would you not like to sit up here in front
of me, where you will get a better view?,' he
asked her.

Excited at getting a ride on horseback,
she immediately leapt up in front of him;
her suppleness and strength a total contradiction
of her frail, old appearance. Once she was seated
before him, they rode on and Monroe very
carefully wrapped the hair rope he was using
for a rein around her. It was made from the
hair of a mare's tail and he knew she would
not be able to break free of it. So when she
said she wanted to get down and Monroe just
laughed, she realised that he had her in his
power. He rode back to Lochletter, all the time
the hag wailing and gnashing her teeth, switching
from promising him all kinds of wonderful thing
if he would only let her go to threatening him
with dreadful vengeance if he failed to do so.
All the time Monroe kept a calm demeanour.
When he got home and dismounted, he was
very careful to keep the rope around the hag.
Once he had untied the rein from his horse's

bridle, he pulled her off the horse, dragged her inside the house and tied her to one of the support beams of the roof. He had a mind to try and force her to put her supernatural powers to his own use. Hardly had they got inside the house however, when a terrifying din erupted outside. It seemed as if all the demons of hell had descended on Lochletter at once! As he stood there covering his ears, he became aware that something else was going on. He looked up to see great holes being ripped in his roof as the horde of wild imps outside began to strip his house bare of its thatch.

'Enough, enough!' he cried. 'If you tell them to replace everything, I will let you go.'

The old hag cackled with laughter at him.

'What are you saying, Monroe? I cannot hear you,' she replied.

'Tell them to stop and I will untie you and set you free,' he roared, his mouth just inches from her ear. She looked at him and screeched in a voice even louder than the hellish noise outside, 'Speed, wood and sod to the house of Monroe, except honeysuckle and bird cherry.'

In an instant, all the turf and wood that had been ripped from the house flew into the air and back into the position it had been in before. Then, asking only for her word that she would cause him no harm and getting it, Monroe untied the rope and the hag ran off into the night. And for the rest of his days he would warn all who would listen, never to try and get the better of spirits, elves, fairies or especially hags!

conochar

ong ago in the time of the Picts the Castle of Urquhart was occupied by a man called Conochar Mor Mac Aoidh. There are those who think this may well have been Ochonachar, the founder of the Forbes clan, who slew a great bear that had eaten nine maidens over on Donside. Whoever he was, there are several stories that survive of Big Conochar and one of these tells us how Castle Urquhart was built.

It seems that Conochar was not just a great warrior but that he was a man of knowledge. Somehow he had managed to gain an advantage over the witches who were active around Loch Ness in his time, who regularly met at a rock on the shore of the loch known as An Clarsach, The Harp, on the farm of Tychat. Here they were wont to gather in the presence of their master, Auld Hornie himself. In truly Scottish fashion, once the more macabre business of the meeting was done the Devil would entertain the assembly of witches, sometimes with bagpipes and at others on the harp itself, which is how the rock got its name. Just as Burns described in 'Tam o' Shanter' the hags would loup and dance to the devil's music like teenagers and some of the leaps and spins they made were beyond the abilities of even the greatest athletes. The dark sisterhood would generally carry on their evil ways in secret, but somehow Conochar had gained power over them.

He set them to gather the stone from all around Caiplich and Abriachan for a great castle at Urquhart Point. As they hauled their heavy burdens towards the loch, the first sight they would have of Urquhart Point was from the place since called Cragan nam Mallachd, the Rock of Curses, for whatever power Conochar had over them was the cause of great resentment amongst the witches and they would swear and curse whenever they came in sight of the point. Still they did as they were told and in time Castle Urquhart was raised to command the waters of Loch Ness, and such was Conochar's power that he could withstand all the curses of the witches and went on to have a long and fruitful life secure in his great stronghold overlooking Loch Ness.

conochar's dog

NOTHER WEEL-KENNT LOCAL TALE concerned a favourite hound of Conochar's. It was known as An Cu Mor, the Big Dog, and was of an extraordinary size. In its prime, coursing through the mountains and glens with his master, hunting deer and wild boar, there was no dog anywhere that was a match for An Cu Mor. Its great size and strength was matched by its speed and intelligence. For many years it was a faithful companion to Big Conochar as he hunted the hills around Loch Ness. But all things must pass and when the time came that age came on him, An Cu Mor was no longer the magnificent beast he once was. His hair grew grey and his strength began to fail him. Another hunting dog took his place at Conochar's side and An Cu Mor went less and less from the site of Castle Urquhart till at last he never went beyond the wooden walls of the fort overlooking the great loch. Although it saddened him, Conochar decided that it was time that An Cu Mor should be put down. Although it had been his faithful

companion for many years, it was of no use
to him and though this saddened him there
was nothing he could do about the passing of
time. It seemed that the dog itself too was
saddened at the passing of its former powers
and just lay around listlessly near to the fire,
day after day. Maybe watching the once-proud
animal, lazing by the fire when it used to course
the hills for days on end, reminded Conochar
of his own mortality. We can never know, but
one day he decided it was time to be rid of An
Cu Mor.

He told those around him of his intention
but Beathag, one of the old women of the
community, said 'Naw, naw, Conochar. Let
the dog live, his own day awaits him and it is
not yet.'

Like all men of his time, Conochar knew
it was usually a good move to listen to the
words of old women. They had seen and learned
much in their long lives and their wisdom and
understanding were known to be of great use
to the community. Also, as Conochar well knew,
many of them had great knowledge of plant and
herb lore, handed down over centuries, and some
of them even had ways of understanding the

future. So it was always a good idea to pay attention to what the old women said.

Anyway, that summer a great boar had been seen in the hills to the north-west of Urquhart and every man who went out to hunt for it had failed to come back. Their fearsomely mangled bodies were found high in the hills and it seemed as if this boar was beyond the skill and power of any man to hunt down and kill. Soon it began to be seen close to Urquhart itself and the women began to fear that it could come close enough to attack the children. Something had to be done, and as the chief, Conochar knew it was up to him.

So he readied himself to go after the great boar. One morning he arose just after dawn, picked three good spears, strapped his shield to his back, belted his sword around his waist and set off to the woods. He had intended taking his current favourite hound with him but when he stepped outside, who was frisking about like a puppy but An Cu Mor. It seemed as if the years had disappeared from him overnight. Excitedly, he ran up to his master and started to lick his hand.

'Woah, boy, easy there now,' said Conochar

with a smile, for the sight of the life in the old
dog made him happy. 'Ah, you want to come
along with me on the hunt, do you?'

By now the dog was leaping up and falling
to its feet, spinning around and leaping up to
try and lick its master again and again. Conochar
was warmed to his heart as he remembered all
the years this fine old hound had worked with
him hunting in the hills and he said, 'Fine, fine,
An Cu Mor. You can come with me this day,
but be warned, it is a fearsome beast we are
after and neither of us may return from such
a hunt.' As he said this he patted the excited
dog on the head and this seemed to calm the
creature down a little.

Still, as they headed off into the forest the
dog scampered around him like a puppy and
the sight made Conochar smile.

Soon they were deep in the hills. Reports
that the great beast was getting ever nearer to
Urquhart were proven right when, within the
hour, turning a corner in a wee glen he knew
well, where the trees formed a dark, cool tunnel
on the hottest of days, Conochar found the boar
right in front of him. It was half as big again as
any he had ever seen before and he barely had

time to ready himself before the beast attacked.
The force of its charge splintered the spear that
Conochar had braced against a handy rock, but
as the great beast tore at him An Cu Mor lunged
at it, grabbing its right rear leg.

Squealing with pain, the boar turned from
Conochar to try and gore the courageous dog
with its tusks. The two animals spun around
and around. Conochar got another spear ready
and as the boar shook An Cu Mor off he lunged
with his spear. Using all his strength he could
barely pierce the skin of the monstrous animal
and back it turned toward him. As it rushed him
again, An Cu Mor once more leapt at the animal
and clamped its teeth into its left rear leg.
The beast's charge splintered Conochar's second
spear and he was thrown up into the air to fall
onto the rocks, winded. As he lay gasping for
breath, An Cu Mor attacked the boar with even
greater ferocity. By now the noble dog was
covered in blood from wounds caused by the
boar's tusks. Despite the blood loss, An Cu Mor's
courage never flinched. The wild boar came at it
again and flipped it up in the air, attempting to
catch the dog on its tusks but missing. The dog
rolled over and over as the boar closed in.

Conochar had managed to regain his breath and taking his last spear ran once more at the beast as it closed in on the severely wounded hound. The poor dog was snarling as the boar attacked, but its right rear leg was folded under it and it could not get out of the way of the charge. Just as the great beast was about to thunder into the dog, Conochar threw himself at it with his spear in both hands. This time the point of the spear went clean through the tough, hairy skin of the great pig. It let out a dreadful roar and swung back towards the man, ripping the spear from his hands. Conochar rolled away and leapt to his feet, drawing his sword as he did so. The animal stood opposite him, only a few feet away, the spear sticking out from its side. Conochar could clearly see that the whole of the spear head and about two hands of the shaft had gone into the creature's body. It was growling with pain as its red eyes focussed on the human before it. Again it rushed. This time however was different. The spear had bit deep into its body and some of the ferocity had gone. Conochar realised that it had slowed down as he jumped to his left and brought his sword down on the creature's great skull. There was

a terrible crack and the creature sprawled to the
ground, sliding forward against a rock as its legs
gave way. But it wasn't finished yet. Just as
Conochar got ready to deliver another blow,
the beast whipped round and rose to its feet.
It was breathing heavily and a great gush of
blood came from the spear wound in its side.
It let out a terrible roar and came again at
Conochar. Somehow it seemed to have regained
its strength and Conochar was bowled over,
taking a deep gash to his left leg. The beast
skidded by and turned again. Conochar couldn't
get to his feet. The blow had given him a dead
leg! The beast took in great gulps of air as it
stared directly at its foe, getting ready for the
final charge.

Conochar struggled to his feet and then saw
a wondrous thing. Completely silently, although
dripping blood and in dreadful pain, An Cu Mor
was creeping up behind the boar, dragging its
useless left leg behind it. Just as the beast pawed
the ground to surge forward again and finish off
this two-legged pest, the brave dog sank its teeth
into the beast's back left leg again. This time the
dog refused to let go. The boar whirled; An Cu
Mor was thrown up in the air but held on.

Round and round the two animals turned,
rolling over on each other, the boar trying to
gore the old dog. Once, twice, three times it
managed to pierce the faithful hound's skin, but
An Cu Mor did not let go.

Conochar by now had managed to get to his
feet. Ignoring the blood dripping from his leg,
he inched his way towards the whirling animals.
Just as he got close, An Cu Mor's strength gave
out and it let go of the boar's leg. The creature
closed in for the kill. It did not even sense the
man behind it as it focussed on this four-legged
pest that had given it such pain. It did not hear
the sound of Conochar's great sword as he
brought it down with all his remaining strength
on its head. Straight through the bone and into
the brain the blade went. The boar dropped like
a stone, dead at Conochar's feet, the sword stuck
in its great skull. Conochar too fell, across the
great hairy body of the slain boar. After a few
minutes he managed to pull himself off the
beast's body and crawl to An Cu Mor. He held
the great dog in his arms as it looked up at him,
clearly breathing its last. Its body was torn to
shreds, but no sound of pain came from the
noble beast. As its life slowly ebbed, the creature

looked into its master's eyes, faithful to the very
last. In later years, Conochar would tell the story
of his faithful dog's final service and he always
finished with these words: 'He was the finest
hound any man ever had and as he passed on
from this life to the next, what I saw in his eyes
was pride. There will never be another dog like
him.' And often, as he himself aged, Conochar
would sit in his great fort on the shore of the
loch, fingering the scars he got in the battle
with the great boar, and thinking fondly on
the dog who certainly had his day.

castle spioradan

OR CENTURIES THE CLANS of the Highlands raided each other to 'lift' cattle. It was the way of the warrior, how the men proved themselves, and the point was to gather booty, usually in the form of cattle, which could then be given away within the clan to increase one's status. One day deep in the winter, a raiding band of 20 Camerons had come into Glenmoriston. They had managed to lift only a few cows and were heading back down towards Loch Ness through the woods. They came down a narrow little glen to a clearing with a lochan in it that blocked their path. The lochan was frozen over and was hemmed in by cliffs on both sides. The ground opened up on the other side of the lochan, where there was a wee house. If they could cross the ice they would save themselves the problem of finding a way around, through the trees and along the cliff tops, but they were not sure if they could cross it with the cattle. As they stood there debating whether or not to risk it, an old woman came out of the house. One of them shouted, 'Hey, mother. Do you know if this ice is thick enough to bear our weight?'

The old woman looked up and realised that this was a band of Camerons out raiding her own folk.

'Och aye,' she called, 'it has been frozen for a while and it is plenty thick enough to take your weight.'

And so it was, until they reached the middle of the pool, where the old woman knew well the ice was thinner. There the combined weight of the 20 men and the half dozen cattle was too much for the ice and it gave way beneath them. The cattle and men plunged into the icy cold waters and the men, weighed down with their weapons and their rapidly soaking plaids, had no chance of survival. The cattle though, tough black beasts of the Highlands, swam ashore. The old woman had enough wits about her to count the number of men who drowned there that day, which is why it got the name of The Pool Of Twenty Men.

There were other raids that led to even greater numbers of dead. Although the inter-clan raiding was an activity that had rules and conventions – for instance, clans over whose lands raiders passed driving cattle would help delay any pursuers for a cut of the spoils – any situation involving large numbers of armed and skilled men can easily turn to tragedy.

Back in the middle of the 15th century, the son of the chief of the Macleans, Hector Buie, led a great raid on the lands of the Camerons, to the east of Ben Nevis, while their chief, Lochiel, was himself away from home. At this point in time, there was a great deal of coming and going between Scotland and Ireland and that summer Lochiel had gone off to Ireland, taking with him a large number of his Cameron clansmen and thus leaving Lochaber relatively unprotected. Maclean's raid was successful in that he and his men gathered a great deal of livestock, but such was the resistance of the Camerons who hadn't gone with their chief that many of them were killed. Realising that Lochiel would want revenge for his dead clansmen, never mind the loss of cattle and other beasts, Hector took a group of hostages from the Cameron lands along with him as he retreated up to Loch Ness. Included amongst them were a couple of Cameron chieftains including Somhairle Cameron of Glen Nevis,

Lochiel's brother-in-law and close friend.
He imprisoned his hostages in Castle Bona
on the shores of Loch Ness, just by where the
River Ness runs out of the loch towards the
Moray Firth.

When Lochiel returned from Ireland to find
that the Cameron lands had been pillaged,
he was furious and thirsted for revenge against
Maclean. On hearing of the hostages who had
been taken however, he stayed his hand.
Gathering together a hand-picked band of the
cream of Cameron clansmen, he sent them off
to the area round Glen Urquhart with specific
instructions.

'Bring me back either Hector Buie's sons,
or others of his immediate family,' he told them.

The Macleans and their allies knew fine
well that Lochiel would be looking for revenge
and were on their guard, but they were
expecting a major invasion and the Cameron
party of around a dozen made their way unseen
into the lands around Glen Urquhart. Here
they were successful in capturing two of Hector
Buie's sons and smuggled them back to their
own territory. Now Lochiel was ready to
march against Hector. He gathered as many of

his clansmen and their friends as he could and marched north with several hundred armed warriors. When Hector heard of his approach he sent a messenger, under a flag of truce, to speak with Lochiel. The message he sent was predictable. 'Come any further and I will kill all the hostages.'

Lochiel however was not to be put off. The Camerons came further on and Hector, realising he was significantly outnumbered and thus incapable of meeting them in open battle, retreated with most of his own clansmen into Castle Bona itself. Here he awaited the arrival of Lochiel, still sure that his threat to kill the hostages would eventually repel the invaders.

A Cameron approached the castle, hands held high to show that he carried no weapons.

'I wish to speak to Hector Buie,' he shouted. 'I have come with a message from Lochiel.'

Hector was summonsed to the castle walls and shouted down.

'What is it that Lochiel wants? I have told him, if he does not leave our lands I will kill the hostages and that is what I intend to do.' Hector shouted.

'Lochiel asks will you exchange the prisoners,

for he has your two sons,' the man shouted back, 'and a dozen other of your people. If you kill our people, they will all die and it will not go well for any of you.'

This shocked Hector. He had been wondering why his sons hadn't joined him. Still, they were Highland warriors and understood the way of things. He mulled things over in his mind. If he did hand over the prisoners, he would get his sons back but there was no guarantee that Lochiel would depart. Even if he did so, it was only a matter of time before he would return. The more Hector thought about the matter the more angry he became. His clever raid while Lochiel was out of the country was not looking so clever now. Nor was his tactic of taking hostages. The more he thought about it the angrier he became till at last, in a blazing fire of anger and hatred for Lochiel, he gave the fateful order.

'Take the prisoners out to the castle walls and kill them all, starting with Somhairle Cameron.'

The prisoners were led out on to the castle walls and there, in sight of their assembled clansmen, their throats were cut and their bodies thrown from the battlements.

The reaction to this was all too predictable.
Lochiel, in a furious rage, hanged Hector's two
sons and the other locals he had captured from
trees in sight of those on the castle walls. By now
the warriors on both sides were lusting for their
enemies' blood. The way of the warrior may
have had its roots in the honour of each
individual man but once their blood was up,
savagery was often the result. In fact, the
Camerons were so incensed that they laid siege
to Castle Bona and such were their numbers that
they managed to break into the castle. Everyone,
every last man, woman and child in the castle
was put to the sword and with them died many
a Cameron warrior too. The castle itself was
burned till only the stone walls stood. In fact,
so much blood was spilt that Castle Bona got
a terrible reputation. It seems that the spirits
of those who were killed before the battle were
so incensed by the stubbornness and brutality
of both Hector and Lochiel that they joined
together to haunt the place and prey on any
traveller unwary enough to spend time within
the hoary old walls of Castle Bona. The eeriness
of the place was so overwhelming that it
acquired a new name, Castle Spioradan,

the Castle of the Spirits, and it became notorious
for the strange sights, sounds and smells that
were associated with it, not only in the hours
of darkness. Soon everyone in the area avoided
the place and travellers were warned never to
go near the haunted spot. For hundreds of years
it was a feared and eerie place till at long last
the old walls were torn down and the ground
dug up to make way for the Caledonian Canal.

REVENGE UPON REVENGE

MUCH HAS BEEN MADE down the years of the Highlander's highly personal sense of honour and adherence to the rules of hospitality. People brought up in clan society were expected to behave honourably, but even within close communities there are always those whose character leads them into criminal behaviour. One particular tale from Glen Urquhart shows this sad fact only too well. In the old times there were various peculiar attributes of clan life. One of these was the acceptance of 'broken men' – those who had been thrown out of other clans – as long as they behaved themselves and accepted the laws and customs of their new clan. Another was the habit of fostering. This mainly applied to the sons of chiefs who were raised either by other families in the clan, or sometimes even by a family in another clan. The reasoning behind this was to effectively give the potential chief an extended family of foster brothers, whose loyalty was legendary in Highland story and song. The ties of blood and kin were strong, but the ties of fostering were seen as being particularly important. However things did not always work out for the best when people raised others' children.

One dark winter's night back in the latter years of the 17th century, the goodwife of Shewglie in Glen Urquhart heard an insistent knocking at her door. Opening the door, she felt the cold blast of the night and by the light of the flickering oil lamp in her hand, she saw a young woman obviously in distress, caused by the fact that she was clearly about to give birth.

'Come in, come in, lassie. Quick, get you by the fire,' she said as she ushered the young lass in and shut the door behind her. The young lass could only nod her thanks as she sank into the chair by the fire, shivering violently. Mrs Grant immediately fetched dry clothes for the young lass and as she helped her take off her soaking clothes, she realised that it wasn't just rain, sleet and snow that had soaked the young lass's clothes. Her waters had burst and the baby was about to come into the world. Like most women of her time, Mrs Grant knew fine what to do and, rousing her husband from his bed, she sent him to fetch a couple of the women from neighbouring houses to help with the birth.

So it was that very same night, not long before the weak winter sun rose in the sky, that a young boy was born at Shewglie. He was a healthy and bonny wee boy but over the next few days, as the stranger grew stronger, a sad, if all too common tale came out. It seemed that the lass had been taken advantage of by a passing piper, who it turned out had been a spy from an enemy clan who had led a raid on her people. A raid in which her own father had been killed. Once she realised she was pregnant, she had left her home in shame. She had been on the road for months, relying on the hospitality of other clans and doing whatever work she could in return for food and a place to sleep. She was adamant that she did not want to keep the child whose father had killed her own beloved parent. It was a sad story but Mrs Grant understood what the lass had gone through and agreed to take in the child and raise him as one of her own. So the lass thanked her and once she was strong enough, she left and was never seen again in the area.

However good intentions do not always lead

to good actions, and sometimes the honour code
of the Highlands was conspicuous by its absence.
So it proved with the young lad born at
Shewglie. Mrs Grant had agreed to raise the
boy and, though she had no children herself,
she did not treat him as her own. She was a
proud and imperious woman, Hannah Fraser,
and though she had made a good match in
James Grant of Shewglie, she was known for
having a bit of a cutting tongue and a very
high sense of her own importance. So it
transpired that though she fed, clothed and
housed the wee boy, he never was christened
or baptised – perhaps because Hannah regretted
her generosity.

The boy, once he was four or five years old,
was sent out to look after the cattle and in time
became known simply as An Gille Dubh nam
Mairt, the Dark Lad of the Cattle. It seems
it was the only name he ever got. Well not
quite – his birth, and the lack of knowing who
his father was, was regularly cast up at him by
the children of the clachan at Shewglie and he
was never really made to feel as if he was one
of the Grants. Several times he asked Hannah
who his mother had been, but all she could,

or maybe would, tell him was that she had come
from Lochaber and was probably a Cameron.
So as he grew, An Gille Dubh felt himself to
be an outsider, a rare occurrence among the
Highland clans where blood and kin meant
so much. If Hannah had truly raised him as her
own child, things would no doubt have turned
out differently.

As he grew into his teens, An Gille Dubh
decided to leave Glen Urquhart. He wanted to
go to Lochaber to try and find out who his
mother was. So it was that one night he simply
crept out of the barn where he usually slept and
headed south. In truth, he wasn't much missed.
Even Hannah's husband James Grant, who had
generally treated the boy well and had made sure
he was given some knowledge of the world, soon
forgot all about him. Down in Lochaber among
the Camerons however, An Gille Dubh had not
forgotten about the Grants. Over the centuries,
there had been many disputes between the
Grants and Camerons, even if at other times
they found themselves fighting on the same side
in clan battles. An Gille Dubh located his
mother's people but, hardly surprisingly, found
it difficult to fit in. However he did have one

valuable asset – he knew the lands of Glen
Urquhart intimately and in particular had
specific knowledge of where the cattle were
at any given time. This was very useful to
a group of his Cameron kin who decided to
make a journey to Glen Urquhart and utilise
his information to 'lift' a big creach, or spoil
of cattle. It didn't take any encouragement at
all from the Camerons to ensure that the young
lad went with them.

It was autumn in 1692 that the Camerons
fell upon Glen Urquhart. They did not come in
the night as was usual. They had waited until
the majority of the men and women had gone
off to the peat moss above the glen, to cut and
stack peat for the coming winter, and then came
down from where they had been hiding in the
hills in the middle of the day. There were only
old people and a few children left in the glen
and they could do nothing against the well-
armed raiders. With An Gille Dubh's expert
guidance they lifted dozens and dozens of cattle
as they moved through the glen. The only
stipulation that he had made was that he did
not want the cattle at Shewglie touched.
He felt a slight sense of gratitude towards James

Grant because of his occasional acts of kindness. The Camerons were happy to oblige – they were getting plenty beasts elsewhere. They herded all the cattle together and headed south through Corribuy, towards their own homes.

Behind them, word was sent to the peat moss and soon the Grants were running back in force. All the men ran to their homes and gathered what arms they had with the intention of heading off after the raiders. Now James Grant of Shewglie was well known for his skill with arms, and had played a significant part in the famous victory over the British Army at Killiecrankie a couple of years earlier, so he was chosen to lead the Glen Urquhart men. However, knowing that the Lochaber men outnumbered his own force, he wanted to wait while they summoned more men from further up the glen.

At this point Hannah stepped in. After many years she was at last pregnant and by now was into her eighth month, though impending motherhood had done little to dull the edge of her tongue. As the men debated whether to send for help or give chase immediately she stepped forward amongst them.

'I will follow the Lochaber men, James

Grant, and you can stay home and spin the wheel!' she shouted at him.

This was a terrible thing to do. She was effectively accusing her own husband of being a coward in front of the entire community. The fact that she was so heavily pregnant just made matters worse. James knew well that if he did not set off there and then, his wife's words would be repeated endlessly and he would be shamed as a coward. His anger would have to wait. He headed off with his small force and, as the Lochaber men were having to herd the cattle, they soon caught up with them near Corribuy, at a small plateau known by the ominous name of Carn Mharb Daoine, the Rock of the Dead Men. Seeing them coming, the Camerons gathered together to face them. As the Grants came running up, An Gille Dubh stepped forward.

'I did not expect that you would be here to lift cattle in Glen Urquhart,' Grant said, his eyes flickering along the line of the heavily armed Camerons.

'Nor I that you would be the one to follow me, seeing as I have taken none of yours,' replied An Gille Dubh.

The atmosphere was tense. The Camerons
realised that they had the greater numbers,
but there were many precedents for avoiding
bloodshed if both sides wanted it. So
negotiations were entered into and, by giving up
a number of their cattle, the Glen Urquhart men
were allowed to gather in the rest and head back
towards home. The reasoning of the Camerons
was that it was better to make a small profit and
all return home than make a larger profit but at
the cost of a few lives – even if they had the
greater numbers, such was the ferocity of fighting
among Highlanders that some would surely die.

So, grumbling at the treachery involved, the
Glen Urquhart men headed back down the hill.
They had gone just a few paces when a hare
started out of the heather and ran up the hill
towards the Camerons. Unthinkingly, one of the
Urquhart men, one Kenneth MacDonald, whirled
round, raised his gun and fired at the hare.
He missed. But the Lochaber men turning at
the noise saw a man pointing a gun at them.
At once, several of them began to fire at the
Glen Urquhart men. Having fired their guns,
the Lochaber men threw them to one side, drew
their swords then, with the advantage of the

slope, charged down the hill to attack the Glen
Urquhart band. The cattle, upset by the noise,
scattered down the hill. The fighting was
desperate and though a handful of Camerons fell,
they were too many for their foes, who were
forced to retreat, leaving eight of their number
dead in the heather. One of them was James
Grant of Shewglie. Angered at what they saw as
underhanded behaviour, the Camerons, once they
had rounded up the cattle, came back into Glen
Urquhart to lift the cattle remaining at Shewglie.

Having heard of her husband's death,
Hannah Fraser was in a terrible state and when
she saw the Camerons returning with An Gille
Dubh, she pleaded with him to leave her cattle.

'Remember!' she cried, 'Remember that I
gave you a home. I was a friend to you. Now I
am a widow and about to become the mother
of a fatherless child.'

An Gille Dubh had no intention of showing
any mercy. He remembered the misery of his
childhood among the Grants all too well.

'If you are with child,' he spat, 'bear a foal.'

As Hannah fell to her knees wailing, the
raiders rounded up every last one of her beasts
and headed off to join with the rest of the herd,

now well into the hills to the south. The events of that day were known after as the Raid of Inchbrine and commemorated in a lament that was long sung in the area.

Perhaps it was the repetition of the lament, or maybe it was just the nature of Highland society, but the son that Hannah bore not long after dreamed all through his childhood of avenging the death of his father and the harsh treatment of his mother. With the help of the Grants and his cousins among the Frasers, life was not too hard for young Grant but he remembered that the Raid of Inchbrine was not just the work of the Camerons – they were traditional enemies after all – but had been brought about by the man who had been raised in his own home at Shewglie. When at last he became a man, he had only one thing on his mind.

One autumn evening when he was 17 years old, he headed on horseback towards Lochaber. Word had come to the Grants of where An Gille Dubh was now living. Late in the evening a day or so later, Grant approached the house and dismounting from his horse, calmly knocked on the door.

A powerful looking, dark man with grey-streaked hair opened the door.

'I am passing through the area,' said the young man, 'and ask that I may be given shelter for the night.'

'That you may have and welcome,' replied the man in the door, though his stern look suggested it was not entirely to his liking. Still, it was the way of things to give hospitality to travellers and after a simple meal of venison, he unplugged the old Greybeard, or big bottle, of whisky and they had a drink. The young man was a charming guest, telling of events happening up in the Highland capital of Inverness, and when he was asked of his own exploits in his youth, An Gille Dubh was happy to tell him. With the whisky firing up his blood, he gave a graphic account of the Raid of Inchbrine. As he finished his tale the young visitor leapt to his feet, drawing his dirk as he did so, and shouted, 'The hour of vengeance is now come upon you.'

Taken aback at this, the older man gasped, 'Who are you?'

'I am the foal that the goodwife of Shewglie carried on the day of that raid!' roared the young man, and as he did so he buried his dirk in the heart of his host. He ran from the house and, mounting his horse, rode off into the night and was well on his way home before the dawn light fell on the lifeless body of An Gille Dubh nam Mairt.

a true lover

OW ALL SOCIETIES AT ALL TIMES have had love stories. Along with epic battle tales, stories of the supernatural and accounts of heroes, love stories are a part of the common culture of humanity; they reflect important aspects of just who we are. The people of Loch Ness were no different and there was one tale that was told time and again that is one of absolute devotion. It is the story of Donald Donn MacDonald from Bohuntine in Glen Roy, just to the north of Ben Nevis.

Like most of his compatriots in the second half of the 17th century, Donald was fond of going out on a spreach, or cattle raid. However, he had one particular talent that marked him out and gave him standing amongst not just his own kin, but the whole of Highland society. Donald was a fine poet and bards, as they were known, had always had a respected position in Highland society. The combination of martial skills and the poetic spirit has been valued in warrior societies throughout the history of the human species, and in Donald the combination rang true. He was renowned for being a man of honour, never having injured a poor man or spilt blood needlessly. Along with his immediate kin, particularly his brother Iain and his neighbours the Camerons, Donald Donn ranged over a great swathe of the Highlands, from Breadalbane in the south to Caithness in the north and the lands of Mar in the east.

As an example of his character, a story is told that one time he and his companions were driving home a herd of cattle that they had lifted near Braemar. As usual, they had come down in the night to take their prey and by dawn were many miles off on the way back towards Bohuntine. As the dawn came up, Donald was standing on the shoulder of a hill, looking at the herd of cattle being driven up towards him by the rest of the band. He noticed something a little strange. One of the cattle seemed to have an odd shadow on its body. As the cattle came by him he looked closer. Imagine his astonishment when he realised that the shadow was in fact a woman hanging on for dear life to the neck of the cow. She had clearly been hanging on to the beast since they had left the Braemar area!

'Hey, woman, whatever are you doing?' he shouted.

Realising that the game was up, the woman let go of the cow and stood up to face Donald. The rest of the band stopped the cattle moving and looked on with interest. Now he could see her clearly it was obvious that she was poor; her clothes were threadbare. But what astounded our bard was that her lined face and pure white hair made it very clear that she was a woman well past 60.

'Good heavens, mother!' said Donald, not knowing whether to laugh or cry at the sight of her. 'Whatever do you think you are doing?'

Drawing herself up to her full height, which was not much at all, the woman answered in a defiant tone, 'It is always the same with you men. Lifting cattle to show off to each other with never a thought of the harm you might be doing. This cow is all I have. I am a widow and have no children living. My cow Morag keeps me in milk and cheese, and I have few pleasures in life. Without this cow I may as well lie down and die.'

As she delivered this defiant little speech she was absent-mindedly rubbing the cow's back and

Donald realised that she considered this cow
more than just a means of providing sustenance.
This lonely old woman appeared to have some
sort of feelings for the beast. This was something
that had never crossed Donald's mind, that
someone could have feelings for a cow. A hound
certainly, or a horse – but a cow! He had never
heard of this. Sure, children sometimes made
pets of calves but as the creatures grew they
were soon abandoned and despite their value,
most folk just thought of their cattle as rather
stupid creatures. The thought made him smile
and he knew what he must do.

'Well then, mother, you seem to be very fond
of your cow. Morag, is it?' he asked.

She nodded.

'And you look after it, er, her pretty well,
do you?' he smiled

'I certainly do,' said the woman, still standing
stiff-backed and defiant.

'Well then, mother, do you think you could
look after two as well as one?' he enquired.

Looking at him with a knitted brow and a
puzzled look in her eyes, the old woman shook
her head as if to clear it and asked him,
'Whatever do you mean?'

'I mean,' said Donald laughing aloud, 'I think you should take yourself back to the Braes of Mar with your Morag and that beast next to her.'

The look of amazement on the old woman's face provoked the rest of the band into laughter. The old woman stood there, her head spinning. This wild Lochaber cateran wasn't just giving her back her own cow but another one as well!

'Now, Patrick,' Donald said to one of the onlookers, 'would you see this lady back on her way for a bit, while we press on with the rest? And you could keep a weather eye out for any of her neighbours while you're at it.'

Later that day, a band of Deeside men following the raiders' trail were astonished to be met on the hillside by the old woman walking slowly down the hill with her two cows before her. When they heard of Donald's actions, they were mighty impressed but still pressed on after the Lochaber men. They had no success however and were forced to return empty handed. The old woman was allowed to keep her second cow by general agreement and the Deeside men decided that they would get their own back another day and recompense themselves with a raid on Glen

Roy. Or maybe they would head north and lift some cattle there in the meantime. Such was the way things worked out.

However, the word of Donald Donn's generosity soon spread throughout the Highlands and did his reputation no harm at all. Every so often the Bohuntine men would head north to Sutherland or Ross to acquire some fresh stock and one time on their way north, something happened that was to change Donald's life for ever. He and his brother Iain were travelling along the western shore of Loch Ness, near to Castle Urquhart, in board daylight. The rest of their band were travelling up ahead of them in twos and threes and as they had no intention of raiding the Grants, they felt no need to hide. It was just as he came up to the castle itself that Donald noticed a young woman walking towards him on the road. This was Mary, daughter of Grant of Urquhart, the local chief who lived in the castle. Looking at this black-haired, pale-skinned, young beauty, Donald felt as if he had been hit by a thunderbolt. He didn't even really notice that she was dressed in really fine clothes. She came nearer and he knew he had to speak to her, whipping off his bonnet,

which of course Mary immediately noticed.
But what to say – the great bard of Lochaber
was stuck for words. He simply stood there
twisting his bonnet in his hands, his face flushed
bright red. Mary looked straight at him. She saw
a tall, strong and handsome Highlander. She was
a gorgeous young woman and was used to men's
attention, but this man's speechlessness touched
something in her heart.

'Yes?' she said in soft voice, which seemed to
Donald like the finest sound he had ever heard.

Iain gave him a sharp dig in the ribs,

'P-p-pardon me, miss, but I am Donald Donn
MacDonald of Bohuntine and… and I would like
to know who you are,' he stammered.

Mary had of course heard of the famous
Bard and felt the beginnings of a flush coming
on herself. Quickly she looked away.

'Would that mean you are a poet, sir?'
she said, her head turned away so he would not
notice her heightened colour.

'They do say I have some of the makings of
a bard,' replied Donald, beginning to feel a bit
more like himself, 'but never have I seen such
beauty in the world as that which stands before
me now on the banks of Loch Ness.'

At this Mary flushed even more and she could not resist turning back to look straight into the stranger's eyes.

'Well then, Donald Donn MacDonald. I am Mary, daughter of Seumas, chief of Clan Grant, and I live here in Castle Urquhart. But I have things to be doing,' she said, the look in the handsome man's eyes suddenly making her feel very flustered indeed. 'Perhaps we may meet again.'

'That will happen,' said Donald, his confidence returning.

'Well then good day to you, sir,' she said, nodded at Iain and hurried off to the cattle.

Now Donald had laid his plans and was due to meet up with his companions up the road, so he and Iain pressed on. They were successful in their raid and Iain was in no way surprised when Donald suggested they bring the cattle back down the western side of Loch Ness. Right enough, Donald took the opportunity of going to see Mary and her father, who cottoned on immediately that this MacDonald had fallen for his daughter. Now Donald was a man with a good reputation and he was a famous bard, but Seumas Grant was a very proud man. Every Highland warrior considered himself a true gentleman but Seumas had always intended that Mary, his only daughter, would marry a chief of one of the big clans and so was not at all responsive to Donald's obvious interest. However Donald was not a man to be put off easily and over the next few months he made a series of visits to Castle Urquhart, despite the chief's obvious growing displeasure. In fact after the fourth visit, he made it plain to Donald that he was not welcome and he forbade Mary from ever seeing the Lochaber man again. Donald knew well that his life would be forfeit if he showed up at Castle Urquhart again in direct contravention of Grant's orders, so he tried to put Mary out of his mind but found he couldn't.

All through the following winter he could think of little else and the poems he created were among his best. The following year, he, Iain and the others again raided far to the north and, despite the danger, Donald decided he had to see Mary again. This time the Lochaber men took their cattle much deeper through the hills above Glen Urquhart. They stopped for the night high in the hills and Donald headed down

towards Castle Urquhart. He had an old friend,
a Grant himself and likewise a notable bard,
who lived in Glen Urquhart and in the gloaming
Donald arrived at his house. Despite the chief's
antagonism, Donald's friend was prepared not
just to put him up but to arrange for Mary to
come to his house. So the following day Mary,
who had been pining for Donald as much as he
had for her, came to his house. As their host left
them alone, they fell into each others' arms.
Soon they were discussing the future and Donald
was certain he could find a way to bring her
father round, but Mary was not so sure.

They only had a short time together, for
Donald had to get back to his companions who
had already waited twenty–four hours for him.
It was a fateful delay for it had allowed the men
of the Ross clan, who were tracking them, time
to catch up and just as Donald got back to his
companions, the Rosses fell upon them.
The combined Lochaber force of McDonalds
and Camerons was considerably outnumbered
and in the fight that followed, they lost several
of their number and were forced to flee, leaving
the cattle they had lifted with their original
owners. Donald's dalliance with his love had

been truly expensive. However something
almost as bad came about after the battle.
The Ross men had had a couple of their number
ahead of the main body as scouts and they
had seen Donald head off towards the Loch
and come back the next day. Such was
Donald's reputation that they had heard of
his love for Mary and went to tell Grant of
Urquhart that he had been in the immediate
area of the castle, knowing well that there
could only be one reason.

Grant was furious with his daughter but even
more so with this presumptuous MacDonald.
He sent a large force of Grants after the raiders,
but they were too far ahead and escaped.
Angry that his prey had escaped him, Grant was
at least satisfied that the troublesome poet was
out of reach of his daughter. Or so he thought.

Donald was never a man to be put off by
danger and after meeting Mary had decided
to stay in the area to lay plans for spiriting
her away. He had doubled back to Glen
Urquhart as his kinsmen and their friends
headed home. After her latest liaison with
Donald, Mary began to hope that she might
get her father to change his mind. She was

wrong. Her earlier feelings had been right –
Grant was now obsessed with finding and
killing Donald Donn, who he thought was back
in Lochaber. Donald realised that he couldn't
keep exposing his friend to danger and decided
to hide out in a cave he knew of that overlooked
the Alt-saigh burn. The cave was extremely hard
to find, but given that he was in Grant country
there was little chance that he could remain
undiscovered for long. He knew his fellow bard
would try and let Mary know where he was.
In the meantime, he sneaked out to spy out the
land and try to come up with some plan to get
Mary away from her father. It was inevitable that
he would be noticed and it soon came to the
chief's attention that he was hiding out in the
cave. However the way into the cave was narrow
and exposed and, knowing fine well that Donald
would be fully armed, the chief saw no reason to
lose any men in a frontal assault on the cave.

So it was that one evening Donald heard
someone approach his hideout. Grabbing his
pistols he looked out. Coming up the narrow
path was a young lad of about 11 or 12. The boy
stopped and called out, 'Donald Donn, I have a
message from Mary.'

'Are you on your own, lad?' came the
answer.

'That I am,' replied the boy.

'Well then come ahead,' Donald called
out, but as the boy approached he was looking
down the path to make sure there were no others
with him.

The boy came into the cave and told Donald
that Mary wanted to meet him at the house of
a friend of hers, who she said could be trusted
absolutely.

'Are you sure this is the truth you are telling
me?' asked Donald when the boy had finished.

'Aye, I am telling you that the chief's
daughter wants to meet you this night where
I said,' replied the boy, who had no idea he was
actually setting a trap. He had been told by one
of the women from the castle where to come and
what to say, and had no reason to doubt her.

'Very well then, I thank you,' said Donald
and handed the lad a silver coin for his trouble.

Later that night he made his way by the
moonlight to the house he had been told of.
Arriving there, he knocked on the door and it
was opened by a middle-aged woman who said,
'Come in, come in and sit yourself down, sir.

Herself will not be long in coming. Will you take a glass while you wait?'

He drank one glass and then another when, at a signal from the woman, the door burst open and in piled a group of heavily armed Grants. Donald whipped out one of his pistols and fired. The gun misfired and before he could even draw his sword he was overpowered. In one of his last poems, composed that very night, he tells that there were 63 Grants in and around the house that night – the chief was taking no chances that his prey might escape. He was tied up and dragged off to Urquhart Castle. There, in the great hall, he was thrown at the feet of Seumas Grant, sitting in his great wooden chair before the roaring fire. Mary was nowhere to be seen.

'Well, well, Donald Donn, will you make a poem of this then?' Grant asked with a grim look. 'I told you to have nothing more to do with my daughter. She is far too good for the likes of you. But you have bothered me long enough and tomorrow you will hang.'

Donald, on his knees on the floor with his arms tied behind him, was still defiant. He looked up at Grant and composed a poem on the spot – the last two lines of which have been translated from the Gaelic as;

> The Devil will take the Laird of Grant
> > out of his shoes
> and Donald Donn will not be hanged.

The suggestion he was making in such a remarkable way was that hanging was the fate of a criminal, and not a fitting end for a man such as himself. While he had gone against the express word of the chief of the Grants, he had done nothing criminal and after all he was a man of some substance; he was Donald Donn MacDonald of Bohuntine, the finest poet of his generation. Still Seumas wanted to hang him, but his close kin advised him against it. Such an execution would reflect badly not just on the chief but the whole clan. Better the bard should be given an honourable death, by beheading! That night as he lay awaiting his end, Donald composed several poems, one of which was addressed directly to the chief and ended;

> Tomorrow I shall be on a hill
> Without a head
> Have you no compassion for my
> sorrowful maiden
> My Mary, the fair and tender-eyed.

Grant, however, was adamant. Donald must die.
The following morning virtually the whole of the
Clan assembled around the hill beside Castle
Urquhart to see the bard's end. Amongst them
was the distraught Mary, there by express order
of her hard-hearted father. Donald behaved with
great dignity as he was led forward and made to
kneel. Up swung the executioner's axe, down it
fell and off came the head of Donald Donn.
But then something happened that is talked
of yet. The head rolled a few feet and landed
upright facing Mary. At that point the eyes
opened and those nearby clearly heard Donald's
voice, 'Tog mo cheann, a Mhairi' – 'Mary lift my
head.' Even death could not dim the love that
the Lochaber bard felt for Mary Grant.

samuel cameron

BACK IN THE 17TH CENTURY times were changing. The ancient way of Highland clan life, based on the warrior code of cattle raiding, was still the norm through most of the Highlands but change was on the way. Although the cattle raiding of the tradition was not to finally disappear till the years after Culloden – when the 'lads in the heather' followed their ancestral traditions while being hunted by the red-coated army – as early as the 17th century the old ways were causing problems. While the Highland warriors were happy to carry on their rieving ways, increasingly the Lowland areas abutting the Highlands were coming under the control of a system of law that took no note of ancient ancestral traditions or of a man's sense of honour. The new ways were rigid and enforced by a growing, centralised power, and the officers of the new law saw the cattle 'lifting' of the Highlanders as no more or less than theft. And, it has to be said, even before the new laws were enforced, there were always those whose sense of honour was somewhat flexible. Truth to tell, the

difference between the honourable actions of a
gentleman Highlander and those of a thief could
be difficult to tell apart outside clan society.

So it was that in the late years of the 17th
century the Sheriff of Inverness, MacKenzie of
Kilcoy, had set his face against any and all
raiding. He was known far and wide as the
Shirra Dhu, or Dark Sheriff, and the nickname
had little to do with his colouring, for he was
fair-haired, but more to do with the severity of
sentencing in his court. He had the power of life
and death and was never loath to resort to the
latter as punishment for even the most simple of
crimes. Now he was plagued by one cattle-lifter
in particular.

This was Samuel Cameron, whose clan
were long known for their skills in acquiring
others' cattle, and he was well worthy of his
blood. Such was the clan's fame that the harvest
moon was known in many parts of Scotland
as 'Lochiel's lantern', by the light of which
the clansmen of Lochiel, the chief of the
Camerons, ranged far and wide over Scotland,
taking cattle and other beasts. This was seen
as their absolute right and Samuel, raised to
the tradition, had been on many a raid with

his kinsmen to increase the store of his clan's cattle. However like many another, Samuel was aware that the cattle of the Lowland farmers in the flat lands north of the Highlands were bigger and fatter and thus more valuable than the sturdy black cattle raised in the Highland glens. So he was not averse to lifting cattle from the Moray plain and, truth be told, there were times that more than just cattle went missing.

Samuel based himself in a cave in the Ked Craig, near Abriachan, overlooking Loch Ness, and from here he raided far and wide. So it was that Samuel had become a bit of a pest in Moray and the lands near Inverness itself and the Shirra Dhu was determined to bring him to justice, which meant the end of a rope! One day after raiding near Inverness, Samuel was indeed captured and the Shirra Dhu was delighted when the notorious outlaw was brought to the prison in the Highland capital.

It had taken a dozen men to capture him and no chances were taken when it came time for Samuel to appear in court. He was dragged in great, heavy chains before the Sheriff.

'Well Cameron, you have been found guilty

of theft,' announced the Sheriff after what was
in truth a very short trial. 'I suppose you know
what your sentence will be?'

'Ach, do your worst, you wee bacchle!'
replied Samuel scornfully. The Sheriff almost
exploded with rage at this and could just manage
to pronounce the sentence of death on Cameron.
He was to hang by the neck until dead, a week
from that day. As he left the court, the great
weight of those yards of chains weighing him
down, Samuel kept his head high and directed
a stream of curses at the judge, repeating time
and again that he was just a wee coward.
Mackenzie was furious but, consoling himself
with the fact that he had at last put an end
to Samuel's criminal activities, he began to
calm down.

The night before his execution, Samuel
was loosened briefly from his chains to take
the sacrament from a minister who had been
brought in for the purpose. He had laid his
plans accordingly and, tensing his muscles as
hard as he could, he calmly allowed the yards
of chains to be fastened round him again.
Once the guards had left he relaxed his muscles.
Now there was some give in the chains and he

began to wriggle about till he had some movement. Samuel was a very big man and had a reputation for great strength. Now he had to use his strength as he had never done before. He managed to get enough chain loose to hook it over a protruding stone in his cell. He heaved and heaved. At last, with a dull pop, the link of the chain parted and he began to unwind the yards of metal draped around him. Twice more he had to apply his great strength, his eyes almost popping from his head and the sinews in his neck standing out like hawsers. At last though, he was free of the chains.

He had noted that the great door of his cell could be lifted from its hinges, something the guards thought would take three men or more. They didn't know our Samuel. Taking a deep breath, he knelt with his back to the door, put his fingers under the bottom and began to lift. Sweat poured from him in torrents as he exerted all his power. At last he felt the door begin to shift and this gave him added strength. Up he heaved and over went the door with a thundering crash. It was the middle of the night and only one guard was on duty. When he came running and saw Samuel coming towards him

with a torch in one hand and swinging a length
of chain in the other, he turned and ran. Samuel
quickly ran upstairs to the battlements and
lowered himself over the prison walls with
the chains that had been restricting him for the
past week. Once beyond the prison, he headed
back to his cave near Abriachan and was soon
back to his old ways.

Mackenzie and his men knew roughly where
Cameron was, but the cave, in a highly exposed
spot above a narrow path, was too difficult to
attack. They knew if they attempted to take
him in his lair that some of them would die.
Samuel was known to be a dead shot with both
pistol and gun, and the Sheriff's men waited for
their time. They were sure that Samuel would
make a mistake at some point and had hired
a few spies in the neighbourhood of Abriachan
to tip them off when he had moved out from
his cave. Some of these spies of course were
reporting directly to Samuel, being Camerons
themselves and not at all reluctant to take
money from the government. So it was that
the plans that were laid in Inverness court house
came to nothing.

It so happened that one day McKenzie,

who, like many a Highland laird before and
since, was as fond of hunting as his ancestors
had been, was hunting deer on the slopes of
Abriachan when he chanced upon a narrow
path that lay under a great sheer face. On the
other side was a deeply wooded set of ravines
where he was sure he would find himself a deer.
He had become separated from the two friends
who had come with him and they had laid plans
that if this happened they would meet later in the
inn at Abriachan.

As he carefully guided his horse along the
narrow, exposed path, the Sheriff had no idea
he was being watched. From his position up
above, the eagle-eyed Samuel Cameron had
spotted the horseman as soon as he appeared on
the path. Samuel quickly recognised the stranger.
With a smile, he left his lair and with years of
practice behind him, moved stealthily from rock
to tree, to bush to rock, till he was lying on a
great boulder directly over the path that
Mackenzie was carefully traversing. The first
the Sheriff knew of Cameron's presence was
when he felt himself being grabbed by the neck
and a pistol being pressed to his temple.
He hauled on his reins and the horse stopped,

as did his breath. The hairs on the back of his neck rose when he heard the familiar voice of Samuel Cameron.

'Shirra Dhu, I have you now in my power. I am hunted as a beast from the earth; if I attempt to meet my family, I do it at the peril of being shot by anyone that may please. I cannot be worse off and now, unless you will solemnly swear to reverse my sentence and declare me a free man at the cross of Inverness on Friday first, I will instantly shoot you.'

Mackenzie in truth had little choice. He was entirely at the outlaw's mercy. 'Damn you, Cameron,' he hissed, 'I give you my word.'

At that Cameron let him go and bounded off back up the slope, leaving the dispirited Sheriff to head back to Inverness. Samuel knew his man. Ruthless and strict he may have been, but Mackenzie was at heart still enough of a Highlander never to go back on his word.

So it was that the town of Inverness was all abuzz the following Friday, after the Shirra Dhu publicly read out a pardon for the wild outlaw Samuel Cameron. There were many rumours of bribery and corruption but soon the true story was known and most people thought that Samuel had played a pretty decent trick on his adversary. After all he could have killed him out of hand, there below Ked Crag, but he had stayed his hand.

The Sheriff though had little enough reason to regret his action, for from then on Samuel Cameron gave up the life of a riever and with his considerable ill-gotten gains became a successful farmer himself and raised a large family at Muir of Bunchrew.

coire-na-caorach

MANY HISTORIES OF SCOTLAND tell how the Highlands were essentially a lawless place, constantly subjected to feuds and raiding. The truth of the matter is that the ancient way of the Highlands, that of the warrior clans, had different laws and standards to those we now accept as normal. The idea that the hills were overrun with bandits comes from the times, not so long ago, when the old tribal way of life that had sustained the clans for countless centuries was beginning to crumble in the face of the modern world. But it was not until the last Jacobites were driven from the hills to flee abroad or to be executed in the 1750s that we can truly say that the old ways of the clans finally died.

In the centuries before that, as the law of the land spread north and began to replace the law of the tribe, many of those who held on to the old ways increasingly found themselves up against the law, which was administered by local chiefs and lairds who were ready to adapt to the new ways, mainly because it was to their personal advantage. While it had been the

warrior's way to steal cattle from other clans –
and to always be ready for reprisals, or to fight
to defend what he had taken – under the law
of the king, sitting far off in Edinburgh or even
further off in London after 1603, this was seen
as nothing other than theft. One of the men
around Loch Ness who held on to the old ways
in the face of the changing law was Alexander
MacDonald, or Coire-na-Caorach. His nickname
came from the location of his hideaway, high in
the hills to the west of Fort Augustus. As the
chiefs began to desert their traditional
responsibilities as heads of the extended family
that was the clan, and take on the role of
landlords, aping the so-called aristocracy of
England, time and again they used the law of
the state against those who held to the old ways.
In earlier times, when everyone subscribed to
being a member of the clan or tribe, there was
no need for laws written in books, administered
in courts by men in funny clothes. Even the
traditional clan system of landholding rested
on the warrior way. The term used for
landholding was *a ghlaibh*, by the sword, not
claiming that the land had been so conquered
so much as making it clear that it would be held

by the sword against anyone daring to encroach on clan lands!

When Coire-na-Caorach was a young man, the old ways were still being held to and the chiefs themselves were yet to sell out their heritage. Such was his skill as cateran, or cattle 'lifter', that he became the subject of a bet between the chief of his branch of the MacDonalds, Glengarry, and Lochiel, the chief of the Camerons, who were based around Lochaber to the south east. Coire-na-Caorach's skill was well known but the Camerons had a man who was said to be his match. This was Donald Kennedy or Macourlic, known as An Gaduiehe Dubh, the Dark Thief. Actually, thief is not the correct term but nowadays we have no words to describe the honourable concept of the man capable of taking another's property without being found out! Anyway, one time Lochiel was paying a visit to Glengarry and they were talking about how times were changing fast when the discussion came around to the practice of cattle lifting, and raiding in general.

'Och,' said Glengarry, 'I reckon the finest man to carry out a creach would be Alexander of Coire an Caorach, the man is a marvel. It is said he can pass by within five yards of anyone without being seen, whether it is in the woods or out on the moors.'

'That is as maybe,' replied Lochiel, eager to defend his own kin, 'but I would put Donald Kennedy up against any man in the Highlands. Our people say he moves like the wind through the glens and leaves not a trace behind him.'

'Well then,' said Glengarry, 'we will have to try them out, wouldn't you say?'

'You'll be meaning we should have a wager then?' said Lochiel with a smile.

So a bet was made pitting the clan representatives of MacDonald of Glengarry and Cameron against each other, and toasted with a whisky or three in the traditional manner.

Kennedy and Coire na Caorach were told of the bet and sent into the lands on the other side of Loch Ness to see what they could come back with. They went via Fort Augustus and first of all spied out Glenmoriston, but had no luck finding any untended beasts to lift. It seemed as if all of the Grants were on the lookout and they had to use all their skills to avoid being seen and chased, if not captured. However they were as keen to uphold their respective clans'

honour as their chiefs were and so they decided
to take a look at how things lay in Glen
Urquhart. Things were no better there and
they headed deep into the hills at the head of
Glen Urquhart.

'Ach, I'm fed up with this.' said Kennedy.
'These Frasers and Mackenzies are just too
alert. I'm going to sleep and when I waken I'm
heading home.'

'Whatever you say,' said MacDonald, a wee
smile playing round the corners of his mouth.

Kennedy rolled himself up in his plaid
and lay down in the heather on the hill top,
within moments he was sound asleep. Gently,
very gently, MacDonald unwrapped a couple
of the outer folds of Kennedy's plaid. With
his dirk he cut out a piece of the cloth, just
enough to make himself a pair of leggings.
He then tied them round his sturdy calves and
lay down to sleep alongside his companion.
By now the darkness was coming down and
soon he too was sound asleep. Just before the
dawn he awoke and nudged his companion.
Like all Highlanders used to – following the
teachings of the School of the Moon, as the
cattle raiding ways of the cateran tradition

were known – Kennedy was wide awake immediately, his hand clutching his razor sharp dirk.

'Ach, come on, man,' said MacDonald. 'I don't think there's any reason to be carrying on with this anymore. We might as well just head back, what do you say?'

'I am thinking you have the right of it there,' grunted his companion and without even waiting to eat, the two men headed back south. Later that day they were back in Glen Garry, where Lochiel was still being treated hospitably by his fellow chief.

As they presented themselves, Glengarry asked, 'Well then, you seem to be carrying nothing at all. Have you left beasts outside?' he demanded.

'Ach no,' said Kennedy, 'I think that maybe word of the wager was out. There was no chance to lift anything at all.'

'So you have both come back empty-handed then?' asked Lochiel with a disappointed look.

'Well,' said Coire-na-Caorach, 'I am not exactly empty-handed.'

'What do you mean?' demanded Kennedy, whirling on his companion.

'Take a look at my hose,' replied the smiling Highlander, 'then have a good look at your plaid.'

The bemused Kennedy looked at the leggings then unhitched his plaid from round his shoulders and held it up. There was a hole, just big enough to make a pair of leggings.

At this both Glengarry and Lochiel burst out laughing.

'Well then, Glengarry. I think you have the better of it, right enough.' said Lochiel, and settled the bet.

Even Kennedy was forced to admit he had been outfoxed and, after a few glasses of whisky, he too saw the funny side of it all.

By the time Coire-na-Caorach was into his 40s however, things were changing and the practice of cattle raiding was no longer the norm amongst the clans. Those who followed the ancient, gentlemanly way of life were now seen increasingly as little other than thieves. Truth be told, when such a cateran as MacDonald was ganged up on by his neighbours it meant he was probably raiding far too close to his own home – something that would never have been done in former times. But he had

chosen the life of the raider and it was only
a matter of time before the surrounding lairds
went to the courts in Edinburgh and had Coire-
na-Caorach declared an outlaw. This meant that
there was a price on his head and he was fair
game for any who wanted to attack him.
However enough of the old clan loyalty still
existed among the people of the Loch Ness area
for him to be tipped off as to what the lairds
were up to. He decided that there was no point
in staying in his usual location and went to a
secluded spot to set up home. This was the cave
near the famous Falls of Foyers waterfall on the
eastern shore of Loch Ness. This underground
cave stretched out below the bed of the river
and, capped with a large flagstone, was virtually
impossible to detect.

The cave was 20 yards long but only
had one narrow entrance, under the flagstone
which had a copse of gorse bushes growing
around it, so here he could hide out, safe from
his enemies. He would venture out after dark
and with his 'lifting' and hunting skills, he lived
on the best of fare the area could provide; beef,
lamb and venison. He was also in the habit of
visiting his wife after dark, making sure to be

well away before the dawn lit the sky. This
went on for years and at last the passage of time
began to take its toll on his strength. Living in
the underground cave became more and more
uncomfortable and as old age came on him,
he could no longer venture out and about as
he was used to. At last he became so frail that
his wife, who had got into the habit of visiting
him in the cave, told him that it would be as
well for him to come back to his own home.
Well aware that his end was coming soon,
Coire-na-Caorach agreed. However, the
problem was that by now he could hardly walk
at all and there was no way he would be able
to get himself home. It is often said that behind
every great man there is a fine woman and
though the outlaw was perhaps no truly
exceptional human being, he did have a devoted
wife. So it was that at midnight one night his
devoted spouse wrapped him in a warm blanket,
helped him out through the cave entrance and
tied his frail body to her own back. She then
proceeded to carry him the rough miles to their
own hearth fire, unseen and unheard, arriving
just before dawn. It was only a few days later
that the outlaw breathed his last, lying in his

own bed in his own home. The devotion and commitment of his loving wife had ensured that he died as he had lived, a free man!

the host of the dead

ASTLE HILL SITS OVER the ancient Highland capital of Inverness, strategically located at the north end of the great loch. It is said that long, long ago there was a chapel at the eastern end of the hill on which the castle now sits, and all that now remains is a grassy mound where once the monks chanted their plainsong. Back in that eventful time, when the troops of Cromwell's 'New Model Army' had marched north and occupied so much of Scotland, the church, already then in ruins, had only a low wall surrounding the graveyard that itself surrounded the church. The invaders had come north and occupied the castle and their very presence was resented by the town's inhabitants, as well as all the people of the surrounding area. The well-trained troops were always on the alert, for they well understood the resentment of the locals and that they would take any opportunity they could to drive them from their city. The mutual suspicion and even hatred was made worse by the fact that the Gaelic language, so common

in the streets of Inverness, sounded strange to
the southerners and they always assumed the
worst when the locals could be heard conversing
in their native tongue. Tensions increased with
time and eventually the soldiers, sure that it was
only a matter of time before the populace rose
against them decided to take action.

A party of soldiers was selected to set fire
to Inverness and late one night they quietly
came out from the castle and headed towards
the town. On their way was the old chapel.
Now for centuries local people had been burying
their dead here; some said since Columba first
came to the north and others said that long
before the cross was carried into the glens,
the ancients were laying their dead to rest there.
Whatever may have been the way of it,
generation upon generation of Invernesians
had ended up there. It was a pitch black night
and the soldiers could only see a few feet by
the light of the torches they were carrying.
They were marching in a double column when
suddenly the men in front stopped. This forced
the men behind to bang into them and muffled
grunts and complaints could be heard all along
the column as the force came to a clumsy halt.

The officer in charge, who had been back in the column, rushed to the front, barely managing to keep his voice above a whisper.

'What in God's name is going on?' he throatily demanded as he got to the front of the column. His men were standing stock still, mouths agape and eyes almost popping from their heads. There, by the light of the flickering torches and only a few feet away, was a truly awesome sight.

Not a sound, other than a few whispers from behind the officer, could be heard. The night was still, still as death itself, and there, directly across the way into town, stood a great host. But this was no host of Highland warriors ready to stand against the invader. Nor was it farmers and townsfolk gathered together in their own defence. Sure, some of those the officer could see at the front of the great throng had weapons in their hands, but what weapons! Ancient double-handed broadswords, great wooden clubs, hoary old bows and arrows – but most of that great grey host had no arms at all. Slowly, as he stood there, the hairs prickling on the back of his neck and his blood beginning to turn to ice, the officer realised who faced him and his men. Many of them were no more than skeletons, others had a few wisps of hair hanging limply from their skulls and other had lumps of rotting flesh sticking to their almost bare bones. Not a sound came from that ghastly, grisly gang but all the eyes were focussed on the officer. Beside him his men began falling to their knees in terror, trying vainly to pray to their Lord, for there were many devout Christian men amongst Cromwell's troops, but not a word of prayer could they utter for there on the road before them were the dead of the Chapel kirkyard, risen from their long sleep to defend their descendants from the raid of the English soldiers. The very dead had risen against them.

How long he stood there the officer could never recollect in later years, but as he began to shiver in fear before the great, grey, silent host of the dead he knew he must act.

'B-b-back, men, b-back to the C-C-Castle!' he just managed to croak. And as he took a step back, pulling up a kneeling soldier by the collar, he saw the host inch forward.

'Quickly, men, get back! Get back to the castle, now!' he urged and he began to walk backwards, never daring to take his eyes from the grisly sight before him. His men began to move, clumsily, jerkily, and the host came forward again but this time stopped after a few feet and, as the troops began to turn and run, they simply stood watching. The officer half turned but kept looking over his shoulder as he headed for the castle. His men were flinging away their torches as they went and it seemed to the officer as if a cold, grey, misty light grew around the skeleton corpses of the uncanny host as he began to run to the castle gates. Reaching the opened gates he rushed in. 'Close the gates, now, at once!' he shrieked, the terror beginning to course through his veins. But still he would not give in to that terror. Gritting his teeth and pulling a pistol from his belt, he ran up the stairs to the battlements. As soon as he reached the parapet he looked down into the night. There, in the deep mirk of that cold, dark night, there was nothing. Nothing other than a vague grey mist that even as he watched seemed to draw back into itself, forming an ever smaller cloud over the ancient burial ground till at last, in dead silence, it disappeared and all he could see was darkness. He fell to his knees, his breath coming in great rasps and cold sweat pouring from his brow into his eyes. He ran downstairs. There all his men were sitting or standing, all shivering and all with the same look. It was a look of utter dread. None spoke and as the soldiers who had remained behind came to see what was up, they were struck dumb by the sheer terror they could see on their comrades' faces. They turned to look at the officer who, somehow, calling on all his remaining strength, managed to come out with the words 'Our Father, who art in Heaven...'

As he began to recite the Lord's Prayer, one of the soldiers started to whisper along, then another, and another. As they did so, they fell to their knees, clasped their hands and bowed their heads. Soon the entire detachment was praying in unison and as they did, the paralysing fear that had gripped them began to loosen.

When the prayer was finished, one of the soldiers began to sing a psalm and the others joined in. Within minutes, having heard the singing, the castle chaplain came to find out what was going on and there in the castle he heard of the ghastly experience. For the next few hours he led the men in prayer, giving thanks for escaping from what was clearly an evil host raised by the Devil's hand. Few indeed were the soldiers who slept at all that night, or for the next few nights either, and of those who did many were wracked by nightmares, rousing their friends with wild screams again and again through the night.

And yet, even the most devout or superstitious of men find ways of dealing with reality and within a few days the worst of the fear had passed and talk began again of the need to teach the locals a lesson. Soon indeed the soldiers were accusing the townsfolk of summoning up the Evil One himself. This just fuelled their loathing for the Scots and, despite the horrors of meeting the host of the dead, the talk was soon of the need to do what had been decided on and set the town of Inverness alight. It was God's work, they told each other and the commanding officer took little convincing that they should finish what they had started.

So it was that barely a week after the ghostly encounter at the old Chapel, the same detachment of troops set out in the dark of night to fulfil their mission of burning the town.

As they neared the site of the Chapel they could not help but remember their fears, but this time no ghastly force rose to greet them. Sighing with relief, the officer looked on towards the town. He stopped still and again the column backed up behind him. Men came to the front to see what had happened this time, their weapons clutched tightly in their fists. There they saw a strange site. The whole town of Inverness below them was already in flames. Someone had beaten them to it. Puzzled by this turn of events, the officer returned with his men to the barracks. They would go down and see what was left of the burgh in the morning.

You can imagine their surprise when, on looking out from the castle walls in the morning, the town of Inverness stood as it always had, with not a sign of flame damage anywhere.

This time the soldiers got the message and never again did they try to set fire to the old town, though it must be said their presence was never welcomed.

a Decisive shot

LL AREAS OF THE HIGHLANDS have stories of local men who were involved in heroic deeds on the national stage and Loch Ness-side is no different. In the momentous year of 1689, when the gallant Jacobite John Graham of Claverhouse, Viscount Dundee, raised an army to fight for the Stewart cause there were many Grants from around Loch Ness who went with him and fought at the famous battle of Killiecrankie, or Rinrory as they called it. One of them was Iain a' Chragain who was known for his great skill with the gun, a weapon that had almost completely superseded the traditional bow and arrow by this period. His nickname a' Chragain meant 'of the rocks or crags' and was a direct reference to the amount of time he liked to spend out on the mountainsides hunting deer. Like many another Highlander, Ian's motives were complicated. He, like most Highlanders raised in the cateran tradition, was always happy to go off raiding if time and circumstances allowed but his clan were also loyal to the Scottish House of Stewart and he happily joined

in when Glengarry, the young chief of the
MacDonells, part of the much larger MacDonald
clan, raised a force in his native area to go and
fight for King James.

So on the 27 July, at around seven o'clock
in the evening, he found himself with Glengarry
in the line of battle, on a hillock just to the north
of the pass of Killiecrankie. There were in the
region of 1,800 Highlanders against a British
force under General Mackay of close on 3,500.
It had been a bright sunny day and the Highland
army was waiting till the sun was no longer
directly in their eyes. Now Glengarry at this
point was in discussion with Lochiel, the chief
of the Camerons and a man of significant
reputation. Not only was he known as a great
warrior and a man of fearless disposition, it was
also said that he had that peculiar Highland gift,
the Second Sight. This was the eerie talent of
being able to foretell the future and as those
who have it will tell you, it is far more often
a curse than a gift.

Being well aware of his fellow chief's
reputation in this field, Glengarry decided to
ask him a direct question, knowing that he
would get a straight answer,

'Well then, Lochiel. They would seem to have the better of us in numbers. They outnumber us about two to one.'

'Aye,' replied Lochiel, 'but it is not always numbers that win the day, is it?'

Like many of the Highland chiefs and their kinsmen of the clans, Lochiel believed that the Highlander was worth two of any other fighting man anywhere in the world. Truth to tell, if the Highlanders could find their favoured high ground and mount their fearsome Highland charge down on their enemies, there were few indeed who could stand such an assault. Raised from infancy in the use of their weapons, the clan warriors coming down the mountain side at full tilt was a terrifying sight indeed. They would throw off their plaids and charge the enemy wearing only their shirts – a sight that gave a distinct psychological advantage and a practice that echoed the ancient Caledonian tradition of rushing into battle bare sark, without a shirt, i.e. naked. The charging warriors would fire their pistols or guns at the enemy, drop the firearms in the heather and, without breaking pace, draw their swords and rush into the enemy. With sword in one hand, they held a great wooden targe, or shield, with a long pointed spike on their other forearm. This shield was a weapon by itself, but behind it the other hand held their dirk. Now the dirk was a frightening, multi-purpose weapon and tool; up to a foot long, with three razor-edged sides and almost as deadly as the sword in the hands of a Highlandman.

Glengarry looked at his fellow chief, then over at the massed troops of the British army. 'Well then,' he asked, 'who do you think will win the day?'

Lochiel, well aware of what Glengarry was doing, turned and looked at him with cold, hard eyes for a second before turning back to look at the enemy.

'That side which spills first blood today will win the battle.'

Glengarry looked at Lochiel and then turned to Iain a' Chragain. 'Did you hear what Lochiel just said, Iain?' he asked with a smile.

Just at that point over on the British side, an officer on a big white horse had ridden out in advance of the front line to survey the battle site.

Iain simply nodded, knelt and raised his already loaded gun to his shoulder. The man

on the white horse was over half a mile away.
Iain took aim, held his breath and fired.
The man on the white horse threw up his arms
and fell back from his mount, dead before he
hit the ground.

All along the Highland line the cheers went
up and at a word from their chiefs, the warriors
cast off their plaids and charged the enemy line.
It was a short and brutal fight. So fast was the
Jacobite charge that the Government troops
didn't have time to fix their bayonets to their
guns before the whirling, slashing, half-naked
men of the north were amongst them. Without
their bayonets, the infantry of the British army
were almost defenseless and the battle soon
turned into a rout, in which more than half
of their number were killed. Those who survived
fled south, leaving the Highlanders the victors.

But it was a victory that had a terrible cost.
In the very last minutes of the battle a bullet
took the life of Claverhouse, leaving the rebellion
without a leader and the Jacobite cause with
little hope. It soon fizzled out, especially
after the Highland troops met with fierce
resistance in the village of Dunkeld a day
or two later.

Ian a' Chragain though had a story to tell, and after he had gone to the land of his ancestors, his descendants on Loch Ness-side took great delight in telling all who would listen who it had been who had struck the first and decisive blow in the great Highland victory at Killiecrankie.

trouble at dores
change house

BACK IN THE 18TH CENTURY Scotland had many inns that were known as change houses. There was one close to the wee village of Dores, on the north eastern shore of the Loch. In the middle years of the century this was run by a crippled woman, Hannah Fraser, and her daughter Jean, who being pretty and outgoing was very popular amongst the customers. She was a bonnie and vivacious young woman and worked hard doing as much as she could around the place, given her mother's disabilities. Despite being crippled Hannah was almost always jolly with her customers and like her daughter, happy to be of service. The father had died years before and many of the customers, impressed with the hard work that they put in, felt a great loyalty to the pair of them. However, in the period after Culloden times were hard.

Everyone knew of the barbarity against the Jacobite army after the battle and Dores was, like everywhere else in the Highlands, subjected

to a great deal of hardship at the hands of
the soldiers. The happy wee inn was soon half
deserted and those who did come in, apart from
the often riotous Redcoats, were little inclined
to jollity. In fact, many regular customers kept
out of the place altogether as it was never
possible to know when the soldiery might erupt.
In truth, the high command of the army saw all
of the Highland population as the same; the
general thinking being that if someone wasn't
an active Jacobite, they were a secret supporter.
Even the loyal provost of Inverness had been
beaten up by Cumberland's officers, for no
reason at all.

With the Jacobite army scattered throughout
the Highlands, most people thought it best to
keep their heads down and just try to survive
these difficult times. The main problem was
that the army made no attempt to restrain their
men and they saw the population as fair game.
The situation went on for years and many parts
of the Highlands remained under virtual army
occupation till the mid 1750s.

Being close to the Highland capital, Dores
was regularly visited by troops going to and
from Inverness. Throughout the 1740s many

of these troops were involved in trying to hunt
down the 'men in the heather' – those Jacobites
who had refused to surrender and were living
in the hills, surviving by raiding the Lowlands
or army patrols. They were supported by the
local population but times were generally hard
and the penalties for aiding and abetting the
rebels were usually short and swift, involving
either a sword or a rope!

Hannah and Jean kept their change house
at Dores going throughout the troubled months
after Culloden. They had to serve Redcoats
almost all the time but, in the main, the soldiers
were prepared to pay for their drink and food.
Jean, however, was constantly aware that she
was in danger. She heard plenty stories of how
women had been treated as the army had
rampaged through the Highlands, and she
was careful to try and keep out of harm's way.
She had several close shaves, avoiding the
attentions of drunken soldiers, till one day in
late 1746 her luck ran out. A group of junior
officers were travelling from Inverness to Fort
Augustus and had stopped at Dores for a few
drinks. They had more than a few and soon
they were all drunk. One of them had been

staring at Jean from the moment he had arrived
and every time she had brought more drink
to their table he had been grabbing at her.
She was used to fending off unwanted interest
but this particular man persisted in touching
her even when she had expressly told him to
stop. Some of his fellow officers were urging
him on, after all wasn't this just another
Highland wench and little better than a savage?

As Jean came again to their table, the officer
who was attacking her simply got up and
grabbed her from behind. Lifting her bodily
off the floor, he made for the door that led to
the kitchen of the small building. As his fellows
cheered him on, his intentions were quite
obvious. At this point Hannah, who had been
in the kitchen, came out at the noise. Seeing
the big drunken man struggling with her
daughter, despite her bad leg, she flew at
the officer. Her hands raked down his face,
drawing blood.

'God damn you, you old hag!' the Redcoat
shouted, letting go of Jean and grabbing
at Hannah. As his hands closed around her
throat she had just enough breath to shout,
'Run, Jeannie, run!'

By now the other officers were up from
their seats and as two of them made to grab
at Jean, she twisted out of their reach and ran
through the kitchen door and out the back.
The two officers chased after her but in their
drunken condition she easily outran them and
was off into the heather behind the wee inn.
Back inside, the first officer had lifted Hannah
by the throat and was shaking her like a dog.
He threw her onto the chair she usually sat in
by the fire and squeezed and squeezed with all
his strength. The poor old woman never had
a chance. The burly Redcoat kept squeezing
and screaming curses at the old woman till
long after she was dead. By now Jean was well
away. The couple of local men who had been
in the inn had taken their chance to get away
in the hubbub.

The officers, fired up with drink and angry
that the young lass had escaped, proceeded to
smash up the inn. Then they went to their
horses tethered outside. Once astride their
horses they simply rode south, leaving the
lifeless body of Hannah Fraser lying in the front
room of her own inn. Jean knew nothing of this.
She had taken off into the heather and up into

the hills. She knew she would find safety in
the place that the locals called the 'town of the
freebooters'. This was a spot on the slopes of
Stac na Cathaig where some of the 'men in the
heather' were hiding out. They were regular
visitors to the wee inn at Dores, leaving off
their normal, and illegal, Highland dress
and passing themselves off as local farmhands,
dressed in the lowland garb of hodden grey.
Several of them however had better clothes
and could, when necessary, put on a show
as Lowland gentlemen. The majority of them
were Frasers and a couple of them were cousins
of Jean's. On hearing of her attack, one of
her cousins, Patrick, wanted to go at once to
the inn and kill the offending officers. The leader
of the band, Iain Ban Fraser, 'Fair John',
convinced him they needed to spy out the
land first. So, having changed into hodden
grey clothes, half a dozen of them headed back
to the change house with Jean.

When they got to Dores, they saw a crowd
of local people gathered around the door of the
inn. Jean ran forward and into the building.
Seeing her mother dead in her chair by the fire,
she let out a terrible scream and fainted. Hearing

what had happened from one of the local men
who had been in the inn, Patrick wanted to set
off after the army officers at once.

'No, Patrick. They were all mounted and
will be well ahead of us now. I am thinking
they will not stop till they get to Fort Augustus.
Let us take our time and think what must be
done' Fair John said, looking around the
wreckage of the inn.

With the help of the locals they fixed things
up as best they could but barrels of ale had been
broken open, plates and beakers smashed and
it was obvious that Jean would be unable to
continue running the place as it was. When
she came to she found she had been carried
to the house of a neighbour, and Fair John was
sitting by the side of the bed she was lying on.

'Now, Jean, it is a terrible thing that has
happened to you this day. Those evil Southron
scum have not only killed your mother but they
have ruined the inn and I do not think you can
re-open it,' he said gently as the bonnie young
lass broke into tears.

As he sat there consoling her, Fair John had
an idea; an audacious idea that would take
some carrying off and could not involve Patrick,

who was seething for revenge against the army.
John knew well that there was no way that the
officers concerned could ever be brought to
justice under present conditions, but maybe
something could be done to help Jean.

So it was that late the following day four
horses were seen approaching the military base
at the southern end of Loch Ness, Fort Augustus.
Two of the horses were ridden by men who by
their clothes appeared to be gentlemen; another
by a young woman dressed all in black; and
over the back of the last horse was tied what
was clearly a dead body.

When halted by the sentries at the gate,
the gentleman leading the sad little convoy gave
his name as Alexander Fraser of Drumashie and
said that he wanted to speak to the Duke of
Cumberland himself. Now Alexander was Fair
John's cousin, a staunch government supporter
and at that time half way to Edinburgh on
business, but he was sure none of the soldiers
would know that. At first the guard brought him
an ensign, but he demanded to speak to the
Duke. A lieutenant, then a major came to see
him and at that point he informed the officer
that he was there with the body of a poor old

woman who had been murdered in her own house by one of the Duke's officers. This caused some consternation. John's demeanour suggested clearly that he was a loyal subject seeking redress for a dreadful crime and his stubbornness paid off when at last he was allowed into the fort with the others and taken up towards the Duke's quarters. There he dismounted and the Duke of Cumberland came out. Now this was a man of whom history has had little good to say, but it seems that maybe he did have a conscience. John Fraser showed him Hannah's body and pointed out that her sole surviving relative had not only been deprived of her mother but left destitute as a result of the disgraceful actions of some drunken officers. Now the Duke was aware that there were many rebels hiding out in the hills and realised that it would make sense to avoid offending the 'better sort' of Highland gentlemen, who were prepared to stand by the government even as his troops pillaged their way across the country. So it was that he promised to see to the matter. John and the others were sent down to an inn in Fort Augustus and told to wait there. A few hours later a colonel arrived with a leather bag, which he said he had orders to give to Fraser of Drumashie on behalf of Miss Jean Fraser. He handed the bag over to Fair John while Jean was in a side room with her mother's body. In the bag was enough money to ensure that Hannah could get a decent funeral and the change house could be refurbished and re-stocked. The colonel let it be known that the money had come from the officers concerned in the events at Dores.

So it was that a grimly satisfied John Fraser made his way back with Jean and her mother's body to Dores. There Hannah was buried in the kirkyard and Jean set about rebuilding the business she and her mother had worked so hard to keep going. As for the officers concerned, Cumberland thought it better that they should leave Scotland and be posted abroad. After all, there were plenty of other places in the world where the British army was busy fighting. No one in the army ever found out that it was one of the rebels they were hunting that had pleaded so eloquently for the young inn-keeper from Dores, and when Alexander Fraser in time found out about it, he thought it the wise thing to say nothing. As for Fair John, he went back to the life of the rebel outlaw, for a few years anyway.

a fun day at fort augustus

THE PERIOD AFTER THE DEFEAT of the Jacobite army at Culloden on 16 April 1746 was a dreadful one in the Highlands. Although the army had been mainly made up of troops from Lowland areas of Scotland, the full force of reprisals were unleashed on the Highland population. In the aftermath of the brutality of Culloden, during which prisoners and innocent bystanders were butchered with impunity, the red-coated army spread throughout the highlands and islands on a mission of vengeance. Many stories survive from these dreadful times and it is no exaggeration that the period saw the death of the ancient Highland way of life; a way of life that had grown and adapted but was, in many ways, little different from that of the Iron Age 2,000 years before. Governments in both Edinburgh and London had long wanted to destroy this ancient society with its loyalties to kin and clan and its love of raiding, and now they had their chance. While the Jacobite cause itself carried on as an active force for upwards of 15 years more, the old Highland way of life was now at an end.

All across the mountains and glens, dreadful atrocities took place – all too many of them at the hands of Scots who wanted to show their loyalty to the British government. Vast numbers of cattle, sheep, horses and goats were simply rounded up by the troops and sent to Fort Augustus. Along with this, there was widespread looting and rape. From all across the Highlands herds streamed into the fort, leaving people close to starvation throughout the glens and readying the way for the eventual clearance of the Highland peoples from their ancestral homes. At Fort Augustus dealers arrived from England and the south of Scotland, eager to take advantage of this livestock bonanza. The situation was such that many private soldiers had acquired their own horses and this became such a problem to discipline that an order had to be published that they had to get rid of them or the beasts would be shot. However this was no great punishment because the proceeds of the greatest livestock raid ever to take place in the Highlands were to be divided up amongst the troops who brought the livestock in. It is one of the ironies of 18th century British politics that the Government was continually going on about 'Highland thieves' while they themselves proved much worse!

The upshot of this was that many of the soldiery at Fort Augustus soon found themselves richer than they had ever dreamed. It was an open secret that the gathering of loot had long been a part of army life – and often used to supplement the extremely irregular payment of soldiers' wages – but this was a truly unique situation and most of the Redcoats soon had money to burn. Soldiers of course have a tendency to spend their wealth on things to hand, like drink and women, and the scene seemed set for a great party amongst the British troops, even as the Highlands were cast into a gloom of despair and deprivation.

There was a problem, however. Back in the 18th century, the idea that Scotland's Highland landscape was one of the beauties of the world was not one that had any support outside of the people who lived there. The soaring mountains, many snow capped and majestically bleak; the tumbling rivers and

waterfalls and deep, dark forests were seen
by the troops as depressing. In fact, many of
them fell sick because of this and, despite their
new-found riches and regular supplies of food
and drink, morale amongst the troops centred
on Fort Augustus began to plummet. The
situation was hardly helped by the patrols going
out deeper into the Highlands and away from
the few luxuries that were present in the army
fort. Generally soldiers who had money, food
and drink would be happy men but this was
not proving to be the case.

The commander of the army, the Duke
of Cumberland, was intent on suppressing the
'Highland savages' once and for all and realised
that the collapsing morale could well disrupt his
plans. He therefore had to come up with
something to distract and entertain his men.
So it was that in June he appointed a day for
a bit of sport. He announced that he was going
to give two prizes for horse racing. This was no
race for the trained dragoons with their great
warhorses, or for the officers with their own fine
bred pedigree beasts. No, this was to be a race
for the infantry, the foot soldiers of the army,
and they were to compete on the back of

Highland garrons. These were the small but
extremely sturdy horses that Highlanders had
been using for centuries. These tough little
beasts could survive the harsh winters and
sometimes sweltering summers of the Scottish
Highlands, and their small size belied the fact
they could carry even big men for hours over the
wildest of terrain. Hundreds of garrons had been
gathered up and brought in. The Duke laid
down a set of rules which were guaranteed
to add a bit of fun to the proceedings. The
infantry alone were allowed to enter and most
of them had little, if any experience of horse
riding; certainly not of racing. Further, they had
to ride the horses bareback. With virtually every
soldier having his pockets full of money – and
many of them also quite full with the drink that
their commander had been happy to supply –
there were lots of bets being laid and the entire
garrison looked on as the races started.
Given that the riders were so unused to horses –
and certainly few, if any of them had ever ridden
bareback before – it took quite a while to
organise the first race. But then they were off.
You can imagine the scene when the first race
started with novice jockeys spilling from their

mounts to general laughter and uproar. Only
a handful of the riders who started managed
to finish the course, but they were cheered to
the echo. More drink was taken and a second
race was run, no less hilarious than the first.
The races provided a focus for what had turned
out to be a riotous day of fun for the entire
army. As the day wore on, some of the officers
decided that they too should have a go and
there were a number of private races run;
again on Highland garrons and again bareback,
with bets of as much as 20 guineas –
a considerable sum in those days – and even
colonels and generals taking part. In addition,
a whole series of foot races were organised and
it was here that even more fun developed.

In the 18th century, it was not uncommon
for even some foot soldiers to have their wives
or sweethearts accompanying the army, and they
were not left out. There were a whole series of
foot races run for both men and women, but
then an officer suggested there should be a horse
race for 'the ladies', referring to the common
soldiers' women. Another mentioned that they
were hardly ladies, to general laughter from
the officers present. So it transpired that a horse

race was set up for women. In those days it was considered impolite for any woman to ride other than side-saddle, but as these women were mere camp-followers the suggestion was that they should ride bareback and sitting astride the ponies as the men had done. By now, with the drink flowing and an air of general merriment, the idea of the riding bareback was also reconsidered. The stories that have come down tell us that the women did indeed ride bareback in their race, only it wasn't only the horses that were bareback. Just as the horses had no saddles, so the women astride them had no clothes! It was a veritable procession of Lady Godivas. This, of course, was hugely enjoyed by the gathered troops and the race itself was won by the wife of a private in the Old Buffs. She was greatly applauded both for her skill and her form and gracefully received her prize which was, appropriately enough, a fine linen smock as well as a silver plate. Suffice it to say that while the General Order Book of the army does mention this race, it is only the horses that are said to have been bareback.

So, as the people of the Highlands suffered their crops being destroyed, their cattle and other stock being 'appropriated' and their houses being burned down by troops who could loot, rape and kill with impunity, the British Army were rewarded with a grand day out at Fort Augustus, laid on by their commander-in-chief, the Duke of Cumberland.

the devil on
loch ness-side

 OW IN SCOTTISH FOLKLORE the Devil is generally treated as a relatively familiar figure. The stories that we have hardly present him as Satan, the personification of all evil, and in fact he is, although malicious, quite often seen as little more than a mischievous and bothersome sprite, rather than a fearsome supernatural horror. One of the best known examples of the Devil in Scottish tradition is of course the piper in Robert Burns' superb comic poem 'Tam o' Shanter' where, although consorting with a group of witches in a macabre deserted kirk, his main function is to play the bagpipes. The various titles he has in Scots attest to this mischievous familiarity, with such terms as Auld Hornie and Auld Clootie testifying to the familiarity with which he was treated. In Loch Ness Gaelic tradition he had three forms: black, speckled and white. One tale from Loch Ness-side gives a perfect instance of the almost commonplace attitude towards the Devil.

It concerns a husband and wife at Invermoriston who, when they married, were both considered to be even-tempered and gracious. Such was their temperament that both were highly thought of in the local community and great things were expected of their marriage. However, things do not always develop as expected and soon the people around Invermoriston were taken aback to find that this pair of generous and pleasant people were almost permanently at each other's throats. Even when in public, they would quarrel and this was a great scandal. Several of their friends tried to help them to get on better but to no avail. Of course, in those olden times, once you were married, you were married for life – unless one of you died first. Divorce was unheard of and even if it did take place, which was usually amongst the much better-off, it was always a cause of great disapproval amongst the general community.

One time, after a particularly bad public row between the pair which had the whole parish gossiping furiously, a friend of the couple decided he had to try and do something, even if all efforts to date had failed.

So one evening he headed to their house, set on at least getting them to listen to what he had to tell them about how they were scandalizing their neighbours with their constant bickering. As he approached their home he could hear them shouting at each other from nearly a hundred yards off. Knitting his brows, he hurried on and as he got to the house he looked in the window. There they were, the pair of them, standing face to face, shouting at each other. However, maybe it was because of a kink in the glass or perhaps it was the light at that time of the evening, but he could see that the unhappy couple were not on their own. Standing beside them was a repulsive looking, misshapen beast of a creature; dark of skin and with a long barbed tale. If the husband stopped shouting for a second the creature seemed to give him a nip, and if the wife halted her stream of imprecations at her husband, it looked like he was scratching her with his long pointed nails. Neither of them seemed to be at all aware of the creature's presence.

At first the watcher's blood ran cold as he realised this could be none but Auld Hornie himself, pushing and provoking the couple into ever greater insults at each other. However, he was a man of considerable strength of character and taking a deep breath, he went to the door and, without knocking, turned the handle and stepped into the room. Because he had already seen the fiend, he could still make him out. The evil monster had turned to stare at him. At once he fell to his knees and said, 'Now join me in prayer and stop your quarrelling.' Both man and wife, taken aback by the sudden appearance of their friend, did as he told them and fell to their knees, clasping their hands in front of them.

'Our Father…' intoned the intruder, and before he could get any further there was a terrible screeching and the foul beast flew into the fire and up out of the chimney. The man and wife looked at each other, then at their friend.

'Well, dear friends,' he said with a smile, 'I came to try and get you to stop your bickering but that noise you heard was the Evil One himself, for he is the one that has been making you fight so badly.'

The pair looked at each other and in an instant were in each other's arms. All at once they realised what had been happening, and once

they had forgiven each other they thanked their
friend for his invaluable assistance and it is
said that never again was an angry word heard
in that house.

Not all encounters with the Devil ended
so well, however. In the later years of the 17th
century, again in the Invermoriston area, there
was a local man who had a run in with Auld
Hornie that did not turn out nearly so happily.
The man is remembered as Eobhan Ban a'
Bhocain, Fair Ewan of the Goblin. It seems
that he had somehow allowed himself to
become entrapped in the service of the evil
one and every night he had to give an account
of his day's actions before the cock crew – that
is, before the new dawn arose.

Whatever advantage Ewan had thought he
would get from being in league with the Devil,
things began to pall when every night he had to
rise from his bed to go and address his master.
He tried to avoid keeping the date with the
accursed one, but no matter where he was or
what he was doing, he was under a compulsion
he simply could not shift and every night the
same thing happened, again and again. At last,
wearied out with the constant need to do the

Devils' bidding, he resolved on what he thought
was a good plan. He would emigrate to America.
Many people had done so in the previous few
years, including a couple of his cousins who
had written to him telling him just how good
a life he could have in the new country. And
there, he thought, I will be bothered no more
by Auld Clootie. However, his very first night
onboard ship, who should turn up in his cabin
in the wee small hours of the morning but the
devil himself! And this continued all the time
he was in America. So much so that Ewan
resolved to come home. In truth, he had only
ever left on the chance of being rid of his
burden, for he dearly loved the lands around
Loch Ness.

But on getting back to his own country,
Ewan decided that come hell or high water
he would have things resolved between him
and his dark master. No longer would he be in
constant thrall to him. Accordingly, he gathered
a few of his closest friends and asked them to
come and spend the night in his home. When
they were all gathered, he spoke to them.
'My good friends, I have asked you here to do
me a great service. I have already told you of

how foolish I have been to put myself in the
power of the evil one, but if I can break the spell
I am sure I will be free. So I beg you that
whatever happens here this night, whatever
I may say or do, please, please do not let me
leave this house before dawn.'

His friends agreed and sat with him till the
appointed hour approached. It was usually
around two in the morning that he was
summoned. When that time came, he made
for the door but his friends restrained him.
As he began to struggle and lash out, trying to
bite his companions, they got a rope and tied
him to a heavy wooden chair. It was then that
they heard a sound as if a great wind was
blowing. Louder and louder grew the noise,
till it had turned into a bone-chilling, ear-
bursting shriek and the whole house began to
shake and rattle as if it would break free from
its foundations and fly off into the night! Louder
and louder grew the shrieking, and greater
and greater grew the shaking of the house,
till in desperation the group of friends, by now
shaking with terror themselves, untied the
screaming Ewan from his chair. At once he ran
to the door, opened it and ran off into the dark.

Immediately, the shrieking ceased and the wind dropped. All was still. They all looked at each other, fearful of what they had failed to do. Where had Ewan gone? What had happened to him? All became clear in the light of day when, at noon, poor Ewan's body was found stiff and still on the hillside above the village. For it is true what they say – not only does the Devil drive a hard bargain, but it is a bargain that cannot be broken but by death!

Dulshangie's Contract

OW RELIGION HAS LONG BEEN a bone of contention in Scotland. While the population in general have long been avowedly Christian, the differences in interpretation of what should constitute the actual practice of Christianity have never long been far from the surface of community life. The reformation of the 16th century and the Killing Times of the 17th century are a testament to how divisive religion can be. The entitlement of landowners to appoint the local minister was something that in the 17th and 18th centuries caused a lot of ill feeling in rural and Highland communities.

As the 17th century grew to a close, the parish of Urquhart was the scene of a severe level of disruption in religion. When the well-loved local minister the Reverend James Grant died in 1798, his replacement was Mr James Fowler. Now there was already a movement towards more democratic forms of church organisation spreading through Scotland and Mr Fowler's style, and probably his ideas, were not at all to the taste of many of his parishioners.

In fact, the day that he was due to be inducted
into his new position at Urquhart, violence
was only narrowly averted. Dissatisfaction at
this appointment was widespread and, as was
so often the case in the Highlands, it was the
local women who were to the fore in resisting
what they saw as interference from their
supposed 'betters'. Many of them came to the
church with their aprons full of stones, ready
to physically stop the new man from taking
up his position as their minister. Luckily violence
was avoided but the unhappy locals refused
to attend services led by Mr Fowler and were
soon going off to meetings held by the
charismatic preacher Duncan MacDonald
of Buntait. Now this was seen by some as a
direct affront to the power and authority of
the local Laird and no one felt it more than
the factor, Duncan Grant of Dulshangie,
who happened to be Fowler's brother-in-law.
When he heard that MacDonald was advising
local men not to sign up with the local militia –
instituted by the Government in response to
the fears of sedition and rebellion caused by
the French Revolution – he was furious. His
reaction may have had something to do with

the fact that he was a lieutenant in the militia, and that the local captain was his father-in-law, Alpin Grant of Borlum. He attempted to have MacDonald prosecuted and regularly harangued the local people for insolence and even treason! The more he railed at the locals, the more intransigent they became and soon he was virtually out of control and it became obvious that he was likely to do something foolish. A factor who angers his tenants is not an efficient one and as resentment against him grew, there was talk of rents being withheld. It seemed the tenants of Urquhart were about to break out into open revolt against the factor. This was an intolerable situation and it was soon resolved that he should leave Urquhart. He re-located to Buntait, to work for the chief of the Chisholms, and it was here that the locals say he eventually got what he deserved.

Dulshangie's extreme behaviour and intolerant attitude towards the local community gave rise to the idea that he must be in league with the Devil. No one locally doubted it at all, and all knew that the Devil was a devious master and that no contract with him ever ended well.

It is told that the Devil himself eventually grew tired of Dulshangie and conspired with the local witches to destroy the factor.

One night, he was returning from Inverness with Campbell of Borlum-mor when they came to the woods at Abriachan. As they entered the woods, the moonlight grew weaker and weaker till there was hardly any light at all. Still, they were sure their horses knew the road well and were unconcerned. However, deep in the woods they saw a strange glowing on the path ahead of them. As they approached, they realised that it was none other than the Devil himself standing before them. Both men tried to turn their now terrified horses and flee. Campbell managed to get his animal under control and rode back towards Inverness, Dulshangie was not so lucky. He was held in the power of the Devil as the evil creature approached. He was dragged from his horse and the poor creature, driven mad with terror, galloped off into the thick woods. The Devil then proceeded to beat Dulshangie with cold and calculated venom. It seemed to the desperate factor that the beating went on for hour after hour, and when at last it stopped, he lay in a bloody heap on the road.

He was found at dawn by a couple of local men and taken home to Buntait, where he was put to bed. No one thought that he would survive the terrible beating he had taken, the Devil had arranged '*tae mak siccar Dulshangie wuid dee*' – to make absolutely sure that his victim would not survive. His devoted sisterhood of witches had been busy making a *corp creadh*, a wax image of Dulshangie, with bits of his hair and nail cuttings they had deviously acquired stuck in it. They had then stuck the figure with pins and placed it in a local burn. As the image wore away, so the life ebbed from the body of Duncan Grant. The Devil was making very sure indeed.

The effect of his death on the community was considerable. Many of the locals thought he had got no more then he deserved, and even among those who had accepted his brother-in-law Fowler as their minister, many began to have second thoughts. So it was that in the year of 1803, the minister saw his congregation virtually disappear and soon he was preaching to an almost totally empty kirk. The Laird and his family, and those employed directly in his household, were almost all who would attend

Mr Fowler's services and it was a good few
years before his church even had any elders from
amongst the congregation. It seems that the Devil
too, sometimes works in mysterious ways.

the daft lad

DOWN THE YEARS many unfortunate inhabitants of the shores of Loch Ness ended up spending time in the prison in Inverness. For long enough, the jail was in a four metre square hole inside the main bridge over the river Ness. This dark hole was covered with a grating and was accessed down a flight of stairs. When the prison in the castle was being built, it was used again as a temporary lock up. One of its inhabitants in the latter years of its use was one Alan Cameron from Lochaber, who was arrested for stealing cattle as late as the second decade of the 19th century. Now Alan was generally thought a bit simple and there were those who said that he had been trying to copy the heroes of an old story about the cateran when he was caught lifting the cattle. Be that as it may, Alan was locked up in the old dungeon. As ever in those far off days, the welfare of prisoners was never high on the agenda of the local authorities and those who were locked up generally had to rely on their friends or family to feed them. Alan, far from his own people, had no one to supply him with the necessities of life and depended upon the good graces of the locals. This was, however, a bit of a mixed blessing as mischievous lads and lasses of the town had a habit of playing a trick on anyone in such straits. They would let down bread on a string through the grating and torment prisoners by pulling and jerking on the string. It was a pretty cruel sport but in the end the miscreant usually ended up with the bread and was grateful for it. In fact, so often was this happening that Alan at one point became fed up with what was on offer and called out to his persecutors, 'I'll tak nae oat, naethin but the white bannock!' He had become sated with the standard oatmeal bannock or oatcake and preferred to eat white bread, which some of the better-off children had been tormenting him with. In such ways can the palate be improved. After a while, the new jail was complete and Alan was hauled off there.

Now, at this time there was a great deal of trouble in the countryside as people were being moved off their ancestral lands to be replaced by sheep in a widespread campaign that has become known as the Highland

clearances. Quite a while before that much
of the Lowlands had likewise been cleared of its
rural population, but that in no way diminished
the hardship that was forced on the Highland
people. In many cases throughout the Highland
areas, the local people had been living on the
same land for generations beyond counting but
with the old clan ways long gone, the lairds,
or landlords, saw greater profit in having sheep
on the hills rather than people. Often entire
communities were turfed out; some to live
hand-to-mouth on the coast, others to drift
into the growing cities of Scotland and England,
and many, many more driven from the land
of their birth to countries far over the sea.
That so many of them prospered in such
places as America, Australia, Canada and New
Zealand in no way diminishes the dreadful way
they were treated by the landowners of the time,
with the full backing of the British government.

However, the 'progressive' lairds did not
get it all their own way and there were riots in
many places, including Ross-shire. Because the
courts were on the side of money and influence,
and thus against the people, many of the rioters
ended up being sentenced to prison and so it

was that Alan Cameron found himself with a
company of Ross-shire men who had tried to
defend their homes and families. Having been
told when they arrived that Alan was no more
than an idiot, they paid him little heed.
These Highland lads, used to the fresh air and
healthy life of the bens and glens, were however
in no mood to put up with being imprisoned –
especially as they well understood that the law
was being used against them and for the interests
of the landowners. If the law was unjust, why
should they pay it any mind? If they worked
together and had help from their relatives
outside, they were sure they could make good
their escape and head off on one of the many
emigrant ships that were sailing across the
Atlantic from the Clyde ports.

So they laid their plans. As they had regular
visitors bringing them food, it wasn't too difficult
for a few tools to be smuggled in. At last the
chosen night came and the Ross-shire lads,
over a dozen of them, worked together in total
silence to take the door of their prison cell
completely off its hinges. Quietly laying it down,
they moved down the stairs to the ground floor
entrance of the prison, unaware that Alan had

been watching their every move and was creeping
downstairs behind them. The lock on the main
gate of the prison proved easy to open with the
tools they had and in the dark of the night they
slipped out of the prison and away. Just behind
them came the daft lad they had ignored and
he, like them, disappeared in the night. They
had friends waiting to help them get clean
away. Alan was on his own with only his wits
to rely on, but despite what people thought,
there was nothing wrong with his wits.
He headed back to Lochaber, dug up the money
he had hidden and saying goodbye to the few
cousins he had in the area, he too went off
to Greenock, where he took a ship to North
America, and was never seen in Scotland again.

Some other books published by **LUATH** PRESS

Luath Storyteller: Tales of Edinburgh Castle

Stuart McHardy
ISBN 1 905222 95 5 PBK £5.99

Who was the new-born baby found buried inside the castle walls?

Who sat down to the fateful Black Dinner?

Who was the last prisoner to be held in the dungeons, and what was his crime?

Towering above Edinburgh, on the core of an extinct volcano, sits a grand and forbidding fortress. Edinburgh Castle is one of Scotland's most awe-inspiring and iconic landmarks. A site of human habitation since the Bronze Age, the ever-evolving structure has a rich and varied history and has been of crucial significance, militarily and strategically, for many hundreds of years.

Tales of Edinburgh Castle is a salute to the ancient tradition of storytelling and paints a vivid picture of the castle in bygone times, the rich and varied characters to whom it owes its notoriety, and its central role in Scotland's history and identity.

Luath Storyteller: Tales of the Picts

Stuart McHardy
ISBN 1 84282 097 4 PBK £5.99

For many centuries the people of Scotland have told stories of their ancestors, a mysterious tribe called the Picts. This ancient Celtic-speaking people, who fought off the might of the Roman Empire, are perhaps best known for their Symbol Stones – images carved into standing stones left scattered across Scotland, many of which have their own stories. Here for the first time these tales are gathered together with folk memories of bloody battles, chronicles of warriors and priestesses, saints and supernatural beings. From Shetland to the Border with England, these ancient memories of Scotland's original inhabitants have flourished since the nation's earliest days and now are told afresh, shedding new light on our ancient past.

Luath Storyteller: Highland Myths & Legends

George W Macpherson
ISBN 1 84282 064 8 PBK £5.99

The mythical, the legendary, the true – this is the stuff of stories and storytellers, the preserve of Scotland's ancient oral tradition.

Celtic heroes, fairies, Druids, selkies, sea horses, magicians, giants and Viking invaders – these tales have been told round campfires for centuries and are now told here today. Some of George Macpherson's stories are over 2,500 years old. Strands of these timeless tales cross over and interweave to create a delicate tapestry of Highland Scotland as depicted by its myths and legends.

On the Trail of the Holy Grail

Stuart McHardy
ISBN 1 905222 53 X PBK £7.99

New theories appear and old ideas are re-configured as this remarkable story continues to fascinate and enthrall.

Scholars have long known that the Grail is essentially legendary, a mystic symbol forever sought by those seeking Enlightenment, a quest in which the search is as important as the result. Time and again it has been said that the Grail is a construct of mystical Christian ideas and motifs from the ancient oral tradition of the Celtic-speaking peoples of Britain. There is much to commend this view, but now, drawing on decades of research in his native Scotland, in a major new contribution to the Grail legend, the field historian and folklorist Stuart McHardy traces the origin of the idea of fertility and regeneration back beyond the time of the Celtic warrior tribes of Britain to a truly ancient, physical source.

A physical source as dynamic and awesome today as it was in prehistory when humans first encountered it and began to weave the myths that grew into the Legend of the Holy Grail.

...a refreshingly different approach to the origin of the Grail.
NOTHERN EARTH

On the Trail of Scotland's Myths and Legends

Stuart McHardy

ISBN 1 84282 049 4 PBK £7.99

Mythical animals, supernatural beings, heroes, giants and goddesses come alive and walk Scotland's rich landscape as they did in the time of the Scots, Gaelic and Norse bards of the past.

Visiting over 170 sites across Scotland, Stuart McHardy traces the lore of our ancestors, connecting ancient beliefs with traditions still alive today. Presenting a new picture of who the Scots are and where they have come from, this book provides an insight into a unique tradition of myth, legend and folklore that has marked the language and landscape of Scotland.

The Quest for Arthur

Stuart McHardy

ISBN 1 84282 012 5 HBK £16.99

King Arthur of Camelot and the Knights of the Round Table are enduring romantic figures. A national hero for the Britons, the Welsh and the English alike, Arthur is a potent figure for many.

Historian, storyteller and folklorist Stuart McHardy believes he has uncovered the origins of the true Arthur. He incorporates knowledge of folklore and place-name studies with an archaeological understanding of the sixth century.

This quest leads to the discovery that the enigmatic origins of Arthur lie not in Brittany, England or Wales. Instead they lie in that magic land the ancient Welsh called Y Gogledd, 'The North', the North of Britain, which we now call – Scotland.

[Stuart McHardy's] findings are set to shake established Arthurian thinking.
THE SCOTSMAN

The Quest for the Nine Maidens

Stuart McHardy

ISBN 0 946487 66 9 HBK £16.99

When King Arthur was conveyed to Avalon they were there.

When Odin summoned warriors to Valhalla they were there.

When Apollo was worshipped on Greek mountains they were there.

When Brendan came to the Island of Women they were there.

They tended the Welsh goddess Cerridwen's cauldron on inspiration, and armed the hero Peredur. They are found in Britain, Ireland, Norway, Iceland, Gaul, Greece, Africa and as far afield as South America and Oceania. They are the Nine Maidens – the priestesses of the Mother Goddess.

From the Stone Age to the 21st century, the Nine Maidens come in many forms – Muses, Maenads, Valkyries, seeresses and druidesses. In this book Stuart McHardy traces the Nine Maidens from both Christian and pagan sources, and begins to uncover one of the most ancient and widespread of human institutions.

… [McHardy's] championship of the discredited myth of the 'leylines' is the jewel in this particular crown – he is not some goggle-eyed fanatic.
THE INDEPENDENT

Scots Poems to be read aloud

Collected by Stuart McHardy

ISBN 0 946487 81 2 PBK £5

This personal collection of well-known and not-so-well-known Scots poems to read aloud includes great works of art and simple pieces of questionable 'literary merit'. With an emphasis on humour it's a great companion volume to Tom Atkinson's *Poems to be Read Aloud: A Victorian Drawing Room Entertainment* – 'much borrowed and rarely returned…a book for reading aloud in very good company, preferably after a dram or twa'.

This is a book to encourage the traditional Scottish ceilidh of song and recitation. For those who love poetry it's a wonderful anthology to have to hand, and for all those people who do not normally read poetry, this collection is for you.

Edinburgh & Leith Pub Guide

Stuart McHardy

ISBN 1 906307 80 6 PBK £5.99

The essential guide to the best pubs in Edinburgh and Leith.

Long familiar with Edinburgh and Leith's drinking dens, watering holes, shebeens and dens of iniquity, Stuart McHardy has penned a bible for the booze connoisseur.

Over 170 pubs
12 pub trails plus maps
New section on clubs
Brief guide to Scottish beers and whiskies
Some notes on etiquette

Whether you're here for Hogmanay, a Six Nations weekend, the Festival, just one evening or the rest of your life, this is the companion to slip in your pocket as you venture out in search of the craic.

The Story of Loch Ness

Katharine Stewart

ISBN 1 905222 77 7 PBK £7.99

Known throughout the world for its legendary inhabitant, Loch Ness has inspired folklore and fascination in the hearts of those who visit it for centuries. But what of the characters, the history and the myths which enchanted inhabitants and travellers alike long before the first sightings of the so-called Loch Ness Monster? Katharine Stewart takes us on a journey through the past and the politics, the heroes and villains, and the natural beauties that are the true source of the magic of Loch Ness.

Where did the name Loch Ness come from, and how did Cherry Island come to be? What can be said of the wildlife that makes its home around the loch? Who determined the fate of the Loch Ness valley as we know it today?

Details of these and other books published by Luath Press can be found at:
www.luath.co.uk

Luath Press Limited

committed to publishing well written books worth reading

LUATH PRESS takes its name from Robert Burns, whose little collie Luath (*Gael.,* swift or nimble) tripped up Jean Armour at a wedding and gave him the chance to speak to the woman who was to be his wife and the abiding love of his life. Burns called one of 'The Twa Dogs' Luath after Cuchullin's hunting dog in Ossian's *Fingal.* Luath Press was established in 1981 in the heart of Burns country, and now resides a few steps up the road from Burns' first lodgings on Edinburgh's Royal Mile. Luath offers you distinctive writing with a hint of unexpected pleasures.

Most bookshops in the UK, the US, Canada, Australia, New Zealand and parts of Europe either carry our books in stock or can order them for you. To order direct from us, please send a £sterling cheque, postal order, international money order or your credit card details (number, address of cardholder and expiry date) to us at the address below. Please add post and packing as follows: UK – £1.00 per delivery address; overseas surface mail – £2.50 per delivery address; overseas airmail – £3.50 for the first book to each delivery address, plus £1.00 for each additional book by airmail to the same address. If your order is a gift, we will happily enclose your card or message at no extra charge.

Luath Press Limited
543/2 Castlehill
The Royal Mile
Edinburgh EH1 2ND
Scotland
Telephone: 0131 225 4326 (24 hours)
Fax: 0131 225 4324
email: sales@luath.co.uk
Website: www.luath.co.uk